MADE FOR LOVING YOU

RESCUE MY HEART BOOK #3

KAIT NOLAN

A LETTER TO READERS

Dear Reader,

A quick note before I get to my usual warnings. Ty and Paisley's story comes in two parts. Originally part of a group anthology, *Bad Case of Loving You* recounts Harrison and Ivy's wedding, where Ty and Paisley cross paths again for the first time in eighteen years. You can read *Made For Loving You* without it, but I promise you don't want to miss this meet cute. As such, the short story is included in this volume.

This book is set in the Deep South. As such, it contains a great deal of colorful, colloquial, and occasionally grammatically incorrect language. This is a deliberate choice on my part as an author to most accurately represent the region where I have lived my entire life. This book also contains swearing and pre-marital sex between the lead couple, as those things are part of the realistic lives of characters of this generation, and of many of my readers.

If any of these things are not your cup of tea, please consider that you may not be the right audience for this book. There are scores of other books out there that are written with you in mind. In fact, I've got a list of some of my favorite authors who write on the sweeter side on my website at https://kaitnolan.com/on-the-sweeter-side/

If you choose to stick with me, I hope you enjoy!

Happy reading!

Kait

BAD CASE OF LOVING YOU
A RESCUE MY HEART PREQUEL

She loves weddings

As a romance author, Paisley Parish is a hopeless romantic. Seeing her friends exchange promises of forever does her heart good--even if the whole thing does highlight her own regrettably single status. But that's what cake and champagne are for. She just has to escape the douchecanoe who won't take no for an answer.

He hates weddings

Former Army Ranger Ty Brooks is happy to see his brother-in-arms starting his new life. He just wishes he was out of this monkey suit and miles away from the seemingly endless parade of guests. All this happily ever after isn't for him, but he's determined nothing's going to ruin Harrison and Ivy's special night. Especially the asshat who's cornered one of the female guests.

A blast from the past

The knight in a tux who shows up with a glass of champagne pretending to be Paisley's date is none other than the first love who broke her heart. Ty's older, hotter, and shocked to see her. It's clear the old chemistry is alive and kicking, and as they take a walk down memory lane, so are the feelings they both thought long dead and buried. Will the night be the closure they never got...or the start of a second chance?

"I hate weddings."

Paisley Parish glanced over as a bridesmaid flopped down at the other end of the settee in a cloud of celadon skirts. The blonde slipped off painful-looking heels and began to massage her arches.

Paisley offered her a moue of sympathy. "I

might hate the shoes, but I love weddings themselves. Is there anything more romantic and hopeful than two people vowing to love, honor, and cherish each other forever?" With a sigh, she glanced back at the dance floor, where Ivy and Harrison circled in their own little world.

Her companion grimaced. "I'm kind of soured on the idea after my divorce. My ex seemed to think those vows were more like suggestions than actual promises."

Paisley lifted her glass. "Then he was a douchecanoe, and you are well rid of him."

"He was indeed. But he effectively proved that men are more trouble than they're worth."

"Oh, I don't know. After my second divorce, I figured out that men are glorious, as long as you don't keep them past their expiration date." She sipped her champagne and winked. "The trick is knowing when that is."

But even as she said it, it didn't feel as true as it used to. She was between boyfriends at the moment. In truth, it had been more than a minute since she'd sought one out. Ivy and Harrison were the second perfect pairing to challenge that particular belief.

Two months earlier, Paisley had helped her best friend, Emerson, orchestrate the perfect grand gesture for the love of her life, the world's most perfect unicorn of a guy. Now that they were married and expecting their first child, Paisley was feeling a bit of a pinch in the region of her heart that might have been yearning. If she squinted at it from the side. Emerson and Caleb were the poster couple for *It's never too late!*

It wasn't like she hadn't been looking for forever. She loved love. Hell, after her first one had walked away to pursue duty and honor for Uncle Sam, she'd made a career writing about it. Paisley considered it a point of pride that she hadn't let that broken heart dim her natural optimism. But real men weren't like the larger-than-life heroes of her novels, and she refused to settle for anything less. If that meant she had to kiss a lot of frogs... well, so be it.

She looked back at dance floor, smiling at the sight of Ivy's head nestled against Harrison's broad shoulder. The usually stern lines of the former Army Ranger's face were relaxed in an expression so tender, it made Paisley's throat ache. They gave her hope that somewhere out there was a guy who'd meet her exacting standards. If there was a tiny, tired voice whispering that she'd found and lost him years ago, she ignored it. She'd had more than half a lifetime of practice.

The blonde followed her gaze, her expression softening. "I have to admit, he and Ivy are pretty damned perfect for each other."

"Down to the ground. I couldn't have written them better myself."

Brown eyes brightened with interest. "Are you one of Ivy's writer friends?"

"Guilty." She offered her hand. "I'm Paisley Parish."

"Deanna James. And oh my God, I love your books! They've helped make up for the loss of the douchecanoe. If I could pull Max straight out of the pages of *She Shed Casanova*, I absolutely would."

Paisley laughed. "He was pretty delightful in that toolbelt."

Deanna fanned herself. "And that whole scene with The Door." She said it with the capital letters that particular interlude deserved. "I'm pretty sure there's nothing hotter than a guy in a toolbelt who knows how to use everything on it."

"Oh, girl, if that's your catnip, then you need to get yourself over to YouTube post haste to check out DIWyatt."

"DI what?"

"DIWyatt. He's this contractor who has his own YouTube channel where he talks about how to do different home improvement projects yourself. Can't say that I've ever paid that much attention to what he's teaching, but he is *delicious* in a toolbelt. Plenty of fantasy fodder."

"I will definitely check that out."

"Fantasies aside, you should get back out there. Back in the saddle and all that. Unless the ink on your divorce papers is still wet."

"No, it's been over and done for a while. I've been working on me, you know? Figuring out what I want and who I am. I kind of lost that in my marriage."

"Sensible. Figure that out and don't settle." Paisley's lips curved. "But there's no rule that says you can't have a little fun along the way."

Deanna waved at someone across the reception hall. "Sadly, fun will have to wait. Bridesmaid duties call." She slipped her shoes back on. "It was lovely to meet you."

"And you."

"Good luck with the hunt. There are some real hotties among the groomsmen. A few are taken, but not all of them."

Paisley lifted her champagne in another toast of acknowledgement. As Deanna walked away, Paisley scanned the room looking for those groomsmen. Arriving a bit late, she'd been at the back of the church for the ceremony, so she hadn't seen any of them up-close-and-personal, but even from a distance she could see they filled out their tuxes well. But it wasn't one of them she spotted heading her way.

The guy crossing toward her like a heat-seeking missile had a bright white smile that made her think of toothpaste commercials. Paisley smiled in reflex, wondering if he had potential. She hadn't come here tonight specifically on the prowl, but she wouldn't forego an opportunity if it presented itself. Maybe she'd get lucky.

"Girl, don't you feel bad for looking prettier than the bride?"

Cheesy as far as pickup lines went, but she'd fielded worse. "Ivy is certainly the belle of her own ball tonight. But thank you for the compliment."

Mr. Toothpaste scanned her from head to toe, lingering on her legs. She abruptly uncrossed them so the ruffled hem of her little black dress didn't rise up any higher. Over the years, she'd been hit on by a sufficient number of guys to have a pretty decent radar of the potentials versus the hell nos. She didn't have a good feeling about this one.

"I would looove to take your garter off."

Paisley stiffened. Yeah, no, this wasn't even a

frog. This guy was a full-on toad, and she wanted nothing to do with him. Even without the slurred words, she recognized he was more than half drunk.

Pushing up from the settee, she made to move past him, but he countered.

"Where you going, sweet cheeks?"

He stopped just shy of touching her, but he was very definitely blocking her exit. She'd retreated to this little corner because it gave her a view of all the action and opportunity to eavesdrop on conversations. As a writer, she soaked up snippets of dialogue like a sponge. But just now she was wishing she'd opted to be more social. There was a certain safety in crowds.

"Excuse me. I need to use the restroom."

"Oh now, don't hurry off. We should get to know each other."

For a moment, being cornered by a creep brought up old memories. It wasn't the first time, not by a long shot. And there was no hero waiting in the wings to sweep in and save her this time. She'd stopped looking for one of those years ago. But as she faced down the asshat, she wished the Universe would do her a solid and send someone because she really didn't want to cause a scene.

"FIFTY BUCKS SAYS there's a bun in the oven by the end of the year."

Ty Brooks pulled his attention away from scanning the busy reception hall and arched a brow at his friend. "Are you seriously betting on Harrison's love life?"

Sebastian Donnelly shrugged. "I mean, we've bet on stranger things than this."

That was true enough. In the field, when they'd worked missions involving endless waiting and recon, they'd bet on all kinds of stuff to pass the time. Including which cockroach would make it across their bunker faster. Sometimes that had been the only levity during days or weeks of grueling conditions. None of them were Rangers anymore, but old habits died hard.

Porter Ingram, always the voice of reason, tipped back his beer. "They look happy. That's the important thing."

Ty's gaze skated back to Harrison and Ivy, now executing some kind of complicated twirling dance. Was that The Shag?

His former captain had been through hell. Ivy was his reward for surviving and a big part of why he had. She'd brought him all the way back to himself. Ty never would have imagined the man could be this contented if he hadn't seen it himself.

"Exactly why I proposed the bet," Sebastian argued. "Those two are full steam ahead on their happily ever after. All that stuff we talked about on missions that we'd do when we got out. They've got the marriage thing down. Babies are next."

"You're not wrong," Porter conceded. He would. His own daughter was only a few months old. This trip to Nashville was the first time he and his wife, Maggie, had been away from Faith since she was born.

As the resident single guy, Ty couldn't resist a little ribbing. "You're all opinionated about the way of things. When exactly are you gonna get there with Laurel?"

"Dude, she said yes when I asked her to marry me. Now it's my job to nod and say 'Yes, ma'am' to anything wedding related."

Porter grinned. "Nice to know your Army training in following orders isn't going to waste."

Ty felt his own lips curve as he went back to scanning the room. His friends were happy. Blissfully so. They absolutely deserved to be, and he was grateful the Universe had smiled down on the lot of them. But that kind of happy wasn't for him.

He wanted to get back to Eden's Ridge, to his

cabin in the woods, where he could avoid all this revelry. Where the sight of it didn't punch him in the chest like an armor-piercing round, reminding him of exactly how undeserving he was—as weddings likely would for the rest of his life.

Years ago, right before Ty had shipped off to basic training, he'd been best man when his brother from another mother, Garrett, had married his childhood sweetheart. Garrett and Bethany hadn't been the only ones to take vows that day. Ty had sworn to do everything in his power to protect the friend he'd known and loved from the cradle. To make sure Garrett came home to his wife for the life they'd been planning for years.

He'd failed.

So no. He didn't get to have a happily ever after. He didn't get connection or comfort or love. Those things were for better men.

Even if he'd believed he had a right to them, he didn't have the bandwidth to form new connections. He didn't have it in him to care about anybody new. He had his friends, and they were enough. Them and the job as a deputy in Stone County that had saved his sanity, if not his soul. He protected and served. It was what he knew, who he was.

Because he could no more turn off his inner cop than he could the soldier, Ty continued to scan the room, watching for trouble. He automatically cataloged the guests who were headed toward too much to drink from the open bar. Somebody was gonna have to steal Harrison's uncle's keys, if he didn't end up snoring in on one of the sofas strategically placed around the edges of the room. And if he wasn't mistaken, that cousin of Ivy's was making a bid for some wedding karaoke —an activity the bride had vetoed in advance in no uncertain terms. A cluster of kids, maybe eight or ten, crept their way past the gift table with an eye toward scoring more cake.

But it was the guy in the pin-striped suit who snagged Ty's attention. There was just enough lack of control in his gait to tell Ty he'd had more than his fair share of alcohol. He moved from woman to woman, flashing a too-practiced grin that turned sharp around the edges as he got shot down one after another. An opportunistic predator. Every social function seemed to have one.

"Okay, you have hidden long enough." Laurel Maxwell, Sebastian's fiancée, appeared from the edges of the parquet dance floor. Somewhere during the course of the evening, she'd ditched her shoes. But the lack of extra inches didn't diminish the force of her personality one bit as she grabbed his hands. "I demand a dance!"

Maggie was right behind to claim Porter. "Come on, honey. We're taking advantage and shaking our groove thing before the clock strikes twelve and we turn into pumpkins."

Porter ditched his beer. "Yes, ma'am."

Ty barely noticed as they all headed for the dance floor. He was too busy watching the shark close in on a woman alone in the far corner. Caramel hair spilled down her shoulders in waves. She was seated on some little sofa thing, people watching or maybe resting her feet in those high, high heels. The furniture around her had probably been arranged for cozy conversation. Instead, it acted as a bottleneck, effectively trapping her when the shark approached.

Ty had already begun to edge in that direction as he saw her go stiff, shoving up from her seat. The shark didn't budge, though her body language shouted she wanted nothing to do with him. It was an old, familiar scenario. One that tickled the back of his brain at memories he'd long ago locked away. He hadn't been able to stand by then, and he certainly couldn't now. Intervening with assholes was simply the gentlemanly thing to do.

As he didn't think Harrison would appreciate

a brawl being added to the evening's entertainment, Ty snagged a couple of glasses of champagne from a passing server and strode across the room.

"Excuse me, man."

When the shark startled, Ty took the opportunity to slip by him. "Sorry I took so long. The line at the bar was killer." He offered one of the glasses and nearly dropped it as he looked into familiar brown eyes that had stepped straight out of his past.

PAISLEY BELIEVED in the power of optimism. She even believed in the power of manifesting. But when she'd wished for a rescue, as she'd done so long ago, she hadn't imagined she'd get one from *him*. And yet there he stood, champagne flutes in hand, as if she'd summoned him by will—or longing—alone. Tyson Brooks. The boy she'd loved and lost so many years ago.

He was no boy now. The years and the Army had honed that once lanky body into a weapon of strength and grace. She could see it in the way he moved, in how he held himself. So still, yet so clearly ready for action. And the muscles. Dear

God in heaven, the muscles. Just the sight of those shoulders made her mouth water.

Had he known it was her when he came over here?

She searched his face, seeing the lines of the boy in the shape of it, despite the close-cropped beard and squarer jaw.

No. No, that stunned look of surprise in his hazel eyes made it absolutely clear that he hadn't.

He hadn't known her at all the first time he'd done exactly this, when some younger version of the current asshole had cornered her at the home-coming dance her sophomore year. It had been some kind of fruity punch in his hands then and a button-down shirt with khakis. The tux he wore now marked him as one of the groomsmen, though he'd left the jacket and bowtie somewhere. The collar of his shirt was loosened, the sleeves of his shirt rolled to reveal muscular forearms that were arm porn all by themselves.

Paisley hadn't hesitated at sixteen, and she didn't now. Driven as much by memory as a desire to evict the asshat in no uncertain terms, she moved in, sliding her arms around Ty and pressing against the firm bulk of him as she rose to her toes to brush a kiss over his lips.

She'd only meant to prove her point. To

claim him in a way the asshat couldn't misunderstand. But after only a beat of hesitation, Ty's mouth opened against hers. The taste of him, at once familiar and foreign, opened up memories she'd kept carefully locked away. The boy he'd been had stood stock still that night, his teenaged brain taking time to catch up to the charade. The man wrapped an arm around her, branding her with a kiss that made her the one claimed. Every cell of her body woke up to shout *Yes!*

He dragged her into a riptide of emotion, as then and now fused into a heady cocktail that had her fisting her hands in his shirt, wondering how fast she could strip it off.

She was kissing Ty. Ty, who'd been her first love. Her first lover. The guy who, she could admit in a deep, dark part of her heart, had likely ruined her for all others. The one who'd walked away to pursue a duty she hadn't understood because, for her, nothing could ever be bigger or more important than love. The guy she hadn't seen in eighteen years.

Remembering that she'd started this to prove a point, she managed to ease back, not getting far in his hold. Her lips still tingled from his as she shifted to look up at him. His pupils had blown wide as he stared down at her with undisguised hunger.

"Well, better late than never," she murmured. "I think he's gone."

Those unfairly long-lashed eyes blinked. "Who?"

Delighted that she'd managed to rattle the big, bad military man, Paisley grinned. "It's good to see you again, Ty."

She disentangled herself with some reluctance and instantly regretted the loss of his warmth. "Thanks for the rescue. I apologize to your wife or girlfriend."

He cleared his throat, offering one of the flutes of champagne that he'd miraculously not bobbled. "None to apologize to."

So he was single. Wasn't that...convenient? Had he been the perennial bachelor, or did he have some failed attempts at matrimony in his past like she did?

Paisley accepted the glass, grateful to have something else to wet her throat and keep her mouth from running away from her brain.

Ty lifted his own glass in a half toast. "You're better at that than you were at sixteen. And you were damned good at it then."

She couldn't quite hold in the unladylike snort.

"Well, I've kissed a lot of frogs in my time. You, my dear Tyson, are no frog." And damn if it hadn't almost been worth the eighteen years to taste him again.

"What are you doing here, Paisley?"

She might have been offended at the question if he hadn't looked so truly baffled by her presence. "It's a wedding, sugar. The correct question is 'Bride or groom?' and the answer is bride."

"You know Ivy?"

"We travel in some of the same writers' circles in Nashville. Or did before she moved to be with Harrison. And you are clearly with the groom. Army buddies?"

"We were in the Rangers together."

Rangers. So, he'd gone all the way to Special Forces. "You always did want to be the best of the best. Congratulations."

Something dark and painful flashed in his eyes. Someone else might have missed it, but she'd once known every single one of his expressions.

"I'm not a Ranger anymore. Left the Army a couple years ago."

When he'd enlisted, he'd planned to be a lifer. She imagined Garrett's death had been the thing to change his mind. While she hadn't lived in Cooper's Bend in years, the death of one of its favorite sons had been big, tragic news that had reached her even in Nashville. She didn't know the details and certainly wouldn't ask. Garrett had been closer than a brother to Ty. His loss would've been devastating.

Wanting to circumvent that conversational land mine, she sipped at her drink. "What are you doing these days?"

"Law enforcement."

"I can see that." He'd viewed the world as so very black and white. Did he still, or did his time in the Rangers make him appreciate the gray?

Because she didn't like the shadows creeping into his eyes, she set the champagne flute aside. "It's been forever and a day. How about a dance for old time's sake?" Holding out a hand, she wiggled her fingers. "C'mon, might as well complete the walk down memory lane."

Something else flashed in his eyes at that. Something hot and interested that told her she wasn't the only one who'd been thinking about where that kiss could go.

His strong fingers curled around hers. "Okay. But I've learned a few things in the past couple decades. This time, I get to lead."

Oh, yes please.

~

HAVING Paisley Parish in his arms was a smorgasbord of sensory memories. The scent of her hair was somehow the same and different from the first time he'd danced with her, after she'd laid one on him that long-ago homecoming. He'd fallen a little bit in love and a whole lot of lust with her that night. She was bold and fun and fearless in a way he'd always admired the hell out of. And the two and a half years after had done nothing but sink him deeper.

The silky feel of her skin where her slim hand wrapped around his made him remember those hands. Tucked in his as they took long walks down by the river. Skimming over his cheeks, his shoulders, his chest, and lower as they explored every inch of each other on a warm September night in the back of his truck, as the fireflies winked. He'd thought himself the luckiest bastard on earth, and even now he wasn't entirely sure he'd been wrong. He'd jumped out of planes, run headlong through enemy fire, diffused bombs, and still kissing her was one of the biggest highs he'd ever experienced. As he swayed with her on the edge of the dance floor, close and yet not close enough, he couldn't help but think of doing it again.

"So, am I correct in assuming there is presently not a Mr. Paisley who left you in the lurch tonight? Or do you kiss all your rescuers?"

That painted mouth he'd all but built a shrine to and worshiped in high school curved. "The only one who's ever rescued me was you. And anyway, there hasn't been a Mr. Paisley in quite some time. Two unsuccessful attempts have convinced me that casual is the way to go."

Did she mean she was twice divorced? It didn't fit with how he'd imagined her over the years. "That surprises me. I figured by now you'd be married with a whole brood of kids."

It occurred to him she might still have the kids.

"Nope." She said it simply. No bitterness, no sadness, just a statement of fact.

It made no damned sense to him. Any man should've considered himself fucking lucky to have landed this woman. "What the hell was wrong with them?"

Surprise and something that might have been wistfulness flickered in her eyes before humor drowned it out. "That's a question I asked pretty often, as it happens." She shrugged. "Life doesn't always turn out like we expect."

He sure as hell knew that. But unlike him, life didn't seem to have dimmed her natural optimism.

She still felt bright and vital, like sunshine incarnate. Ty felt himself pulled in just as much as he had been at sixteen, desperate to bask in the glow of her ready smile. If there was a part of him that rejected that, he wasn't strong enough to walk away because if Garrett had been the bass beat of his childhood, Paisley had been the sweet harmony. He'd loved her once—beyond reason. Enough that he'd let her go rather than risk doing to her exactly what Garrett had done to Bethany. Paisley wasn't a girl who had ever been capable of being okay with sharing her life with duty. And he wasn't the kind of man who could shirk his.

Even as the familiar, dark thoughts crowded in, Paisley trailed a finger down his nape and smiled, chasing the shadows away like his own personal Patronus. A Patronus who just might be a siren in disguise. He shivered at the touch.

"Still there," she murmured. "Even after all these years."

He didn't have to ask what. "Chemistry seems pretty basic and fundamental."

She huffed a laugh and pressed just a little closer. "We always had plenty."

That seemed the understatement of the year. She'd all but blown the top of his head off with that kiss, rousing parts of him he'd thought dormant, if not dead entirely. Ty found himself wondering what else she was even better at than she was at sixteen.

"Yeah, I'm wondering, too."

Had he spoken aloud?

Her laugh bubbled over him like champagne. "You didn't have to say a word. I remember that look in your eyes."

It did something to him to have someone read him so easily. Though maybe lust wasn't that difficult to interpret. "You were gorgeous in high school. You grew up even finer. I wouldn't be human if I didn't respond to that." He was feeling very, very human just now.

She paused, those rich coffee eyes searching his. "Curiosity is human."

"I seem to recall you always had a healthy sense of it." She'd wanted to experience everything, hungry to feel and learn and do. Her thirst for life had been infectious. They'd had so many firsts together, and abruptly, he regretted losing touch entirely. But he didn't know how he'd have survived the choices he'd had to make if he'd still had her as part of his life. He'd had to let go of her light to become one of the shadows.

"Still do. I've been curious about you for years. Wondering where you were, what you were doing.

How you turned out." She stroked a hand across his shoulder, down over his pec, her eyes going impossibly darker in appreciation. "Can't say I can argue with the end results."

The Army had forged him into a weapon and honed him to his physical prime. And it had left him broken.

But they weren't talking about that. Paisley didn't know about the ghosts or the regrets. She didn't know about his failures. Maybe, for tonight, he could just focus on the physical, on the nostalgia just being with her evoked. Assuming he wasn't so far gone he was reading this wrong.

As the song ended, Ty didn't loosen his hold. "Do you want to continue this walk down memory lane? Maybe get out of here?"

Awareness and delight swam into her eyes. She squeezed his hand. "I'll get my purse."

"I'd like hash browns, smothered and covered, with two eggs scrambled and a side of toast." Paisley stuck her laminated menu back into the condiment caddy.

Ty smiled at their waitress, an older woman with a beehive of blonde hair that wasn't too far off from the iconic yellow on the diner's sign. Her name tag read *Gloria*, and Paisley decided she needed to go in a book. "I'm feeling adventurous. Hash browns, all the way, and two eggs sunny side up."

"You got it sweet cheeks." As Gloria turned away, she met Paisley's gaze, waggled her brows and blew out a silent puff of air in a message that clearly said, *Oo, girl, he is smokin', and you are one lucky woman.*

She certainly hoped to be before the end of the night.

The sizzle between them hadn't dimmed a watt since they'd left the reception. If anything, it had amped up when they'd slid in on opposite sides of a booth at Waffle House. Exactly where they'd come after the homecoming dance that night.

Paisley wrapped her hands around the mug of coffee, enjoying the warmth between her palms. "I don't think I've been in a Waffle House since high school." Back in Cooper's Bend, it had been the only place open after nine PM, and they'd spent countless late nights talking in a booth just like this one.

"Why not?"

She jerked a shoulder. "I went to college here in Nashville, so there were lots of other options.

And I guess a little because they always made me think of you."

Another one of those shadows flitted through his eyes and had her reaching out to lay a hand over his. "That's not a dig, Ty. I don't think you made the wrong decision in breaking things off back then. It took me a long time to be able to admit that because I missed you like oxygen."

Ty turned his hand up to curl around hers in a gesture at once familiar and new. "If it helps, it was the hardest decision I've ever made. It was never that I didn't care."

"I know." He'd broken her heart into a million little pieces. But with the wisdom of maturity, she understood he'd wanted to save her from the worst possible outcome of the job. She was glad she could look back fondly on that first love and not have it tarnished with the resentment that would have inevitably grown if she'd tried to share him with his duty.

"We had different paths." Stroking a thumb over the rough skin of his hand, she absorbed the sensation of his touch and yearned for more of it. "I can't say I regret that they've crossed again."

His eyes searched hers. "I looked you up."

"What?"

"A long time back, I got curious. Hunted you up on social media, and I found your books."

"Oh." She didn't know what to say about that. She hated talking romance with people she actually knew—at least the ones who weren't confirmed romance readers. The genre caught so much flak from the uneducated, suffering insult and denigration. Even among certain segments of the writing community there was no respect. She didn't think she could stand being dismissed by Ty. Not that he'd be a deliberate asshole about it, but plenty of people were hurtful in their own ignorance.

"I liked them."

Paisley blinked, sure she'd heard him wrong. "Beg your pardon?"

"Your books. I liked them." He said it easily, without a hint of smirk. Like he was really serious.

"You've read my books?" It was a struggle to keep her voice from sliding up an octave.

"Yeah."

Oh. God. How many had he read? Did he realize she'd been writing the many shades of him all these years? Something that was the bastard child of panic and embarrassment lodged beneath her breastbone. Heat crept into her cheeks as she tried to figure out the appropriate response. "You...uh...aren't exactly my target demographic."

Ty shrugged. "They were good to keep for downtime while I was deployed. Uncertainty was my normal, so having that guaranteed happy ending was... comforting. And you write like you talk, so it was a little like having a piece of you back."

The romantic heart she tried so hard not to indulge outside the pages of her manuscripts gave a full-on swoon. All these years, he'd been in the back of her mind, and she'd thought he'd forgotten her. The idea that he hadn't, that she'd been a comfort to him, that he'd carried a piece of her, even when they weren't together, healed a hurt she'd carried for a long, long time.

Gloria arrived with their food, effectively interrupting the moment. And maybe that was for the best before Paisley said or did something to ruin this chance meeting and make it weird.

They dug into their food, and conversation turned to easier things. They stuck to the past, reminiscing about all the wonderful times they'd had together. There'd been many.

Paisley didn't want the night to end, so when the meal was finished and he walked her out to her car, she turned into him, wrapping him in a hug and pressing her lips to his. He tugged her closer, enveloping her against the frigid January night. The kiss was sweet, nostalgic, and tasted too much like the goodbye she wasn't ready for.

"Come home with me, Ty." Her words were a whisper against his mouth.

He hesitated, lifting his head to look down at her, gaze searching.

Knowing she'd only have one shot to make her case, when the girl he'd known would never have made such an offer casually, she pressed ahead. "I don't have any expectations beyond the night. I'm not that girl with stars in her eyes and forever on her mind. I know your life isn't here. I just want you."

She wouldn't be ready for goodbye tomorrow either, but she'd take however much of him he'd give her, consequences be damned. She understood what this was. And what it wasn't.

Ty stepped back, skimming his hands down her arms until his fingers linked with hers. "Lead the way.

Ty trailed Paisley into the house and, riding the wave of lust, turned to press her back against the door, caging her in with his body.

She stretched up against him with a purr. "I like where this is going, but we're going to have to press pause for just a few minutes."

"Why?"

A volley of barking interrupted her response.

"That's why."

The dog came racing around the corner, a blur of tawny fur, its paws slipping on the hardwood floors as it scrambled to get to Paisley. Ty immediately backed off, not sure whether the animal would view him as a threat. With a joyful yip, it launched itself at him, planting its front paws on Ty's chest and trying desperately to lick him.

"There's my total failure as a guard dog," Paisley cooed. "Down. Down, Duke. Mind your manners."

Still vibrating with excitement, Duke plopped his ass down, his baseball bat of a tail wagging ninety to nothing. Definitely part lab. With maybe some shepherd and border collie mixed in. He fixed bright eyes on Ty, and when no pets were immediately forthcoming, he left his sit and butted his head against Ty's palm.

Giving in, he scratched Duke behind his floppy

ears. "Guess I don't have to worry about him trying to eat me."

"My boy has never met a stranger. He loves everybody. Don't you, baby?" Paisley beamed at him, obviously besotted.

Duke leapt up with another happy bark and turned a circle. Ty couldn't help but think he had the same kind of sunny personality as his mistress.

"He's getting dinner late since I was at the wedding. Let me just take care of him, and we can pick back up where we left off. Make yourself at home."

She moved through the house, talking to the dog. Ty heard another door open and then the echo of Duke's bark outside.

Curious, Ty peeked into the room off the entryway. Clearly an office, one wall was covered in bookshelves. A treadmill desk took up a corner, and another more traditional desk held a sleek laptop. A big, comfy chair occupied the little nook by the front window, flanked by a small table, covered in more books. Instead of art, one wall was covered in a dry erase board covered in post-it notes.

Wandering into the living room, he found a warm cozy space, full of color and comfort, with pillows and blankets and art that matched her boisterous personality. All of it bright, as she was.

There were more books here and a dog bed by the fireplace. Built-in cabinetry held a flat-screen TV and an assortment of board games. Well-used by the look of them. The whole space said *come in and stay a while.*

Everywhere he looked, Ty saw signs of her settled, happy life.

His own cabin was such a counterpoint to this oasis of comfort. He'd been renting for more than a year, and he'd done next to nothing to make it his. Hell, he flat didn't have that much stuff. He wasn't used to staying put. To having a place of his own. His entire adult life had been about traveling light and being ready to go at the drop of a hat. It wasn't a habit he'd been able to break. Not that he'd tried that hard. It hadn't mattered. Not when all his effort was going toward getting out of bed every day and putting one foot in front of the other.

He was past the worst of it, but he could admit, standing in her pretty living room, that while he had a roof over his head, he didn't have a home. Not like this.

The punch of discomfort took him by surprise.

What the hell am I doing here?

Maybe this was a mistake. Maybe he should save her one last time and just leave.

Paisley strode into the room, her heels clicking on the hardwoods. "Duke is all squared away with dinner. Now, where were we?" The teasing tone trailed off as she took in his face. Ty watched her slip on a mask and a too-casual voice. "Regrets already?"

For all that things had been complicated between them, they'd never had anything false. Ty didn't like feeling it now. Didn't like knowing he had anything to do with causing those shields to go up. He wondered about her exes and what scars they'd left on that big heart of hers. As she lifted her chin in a defiant move he recognized as her fake-it-til-you-make-it courage, he realized he couldn't do it. He couldn't walk away. Not yet.

So he crossed the room, sliding his hands into the silky fall of her hair. "No regrets," he murmured and kissed her again.

She might not know it, but she was giving him a gift, and he wanted to cherish it. Cherish her.

On a sigh, Paisley melted into him, twining her arms around his neck as she opened for him, ready and eager as she'd always been. That surrender stoked the fires dampened by doubts. Hauling her closer, he angled his mouth to take the kiss deeper. She met every demanding thrust of his tongue with one of his own, urging him on.

She was sweetness and light and everything good he'd never thought to have again, and Ty wanted to drown in her. He chased the sensation, desperate for more.

As tenderness bled into something darker, more savage, Ty wrenched his mouth away. No. No, he wasn't going to unleash his demons on her. Not like this. He was better than that. Pressing his brow to hers as he fought to catch his breath and find some shred of control.

"What's wrong?" Her hands skimmed over his shoulders, soothing, even as she gasped for breath.

God, that touch. How had he managed to forget what she could do to him? Searching for words, he couldn't stop his hands from kneading at her nape, her hip. "It's...been a very long time for me. I'm not sure I can be gentle."

Paisley pulled back, staring up at him with night-dark eyes and kiss-swollen lips. "Then don't."

Ty STARED down at her with hungry eyes, but still he radiated uncertainty. Sweet, sexy man. She could address that.

"I haven't been a virgin for a very long time, as

you well know. I won't break, Ty." She nipped at his mouth, hoping the little sting would reassure him. "Take me."

She felt the moment his tether snapped. He hauled her to her toes, savaging her mouth until she was unbalanced and breathless, as desperate as he was. It was glorious. His big, broad hands were everywhere, sliding beneath the hem of her dress to cup her ass and press her against his straining erection. She wanted skin on skin, wanted the flex and strain of muscle over her, in her. Spearing her hands in his hair, she dragged him closer, feeling a dark satisfaction at his groan.

Tearing his mouth away, Ty trailed it down the column of her throat. His lips were a fever as they claimed her, and she dropped her head back to give him better access.

And she heard the jingle of dog tags.

"Wait," she gasped.

He froze in an instant, proving he still had some control.

"We have approximately ten seconds before *canis interruptus.*"

Ty solved the issue by scooping her up so she could wrap her legs around his waist. "Which way?"

Dizzy at the feel of him behind the fly of his

trousers, she directed him down the hall. He moved fast, those long, muscular legs eating up the distance with just enough time to boot the door shut on Duke.

His confused, mournful bark sounded in the hall.

"Don't mind him, he doesn't know what's happening. I never bring anyone home."

Something flashed in Ty's eyes as he let her slide down his body. Then he was on her again, yanking down the zipper of her dress and peeling her out of it. Paisley had never been more grateful for her choice of underwear.

He took in the black lace with a reverent curse. "You sure as hell didn't have these in high school."

Preening just a little, she did a turn. "You like?"

"Fuck yes."

God, when was the last time a man had looked at her as if she were some kind of goddess? She was going to enjoy this immensely.

He slowed, fingers flicking open the clasp of her bra and drawing it down and away, until the cool air kissed her bare breasts. Her nipples drew taut and achy.

"You always did have the most magnificent breasts." Ty lowered his head and sucked one rosy tip into his mouth, circling it with his tongue.

Feeling an answering tug deep between her legs, she threaded her hands in the hair at his nape to keep him there. His hands roamed south, dipping into her panties and slipping between her drenched folds. His blunt finger was a welcome intrusion against the ache he built with his mouth. Pumping her hips to the rhythm he set, she began to chase the high. He'd always known how to touch her, how to work her into an absolute frenzy. He added a second finger as he began to circle her clit. It was too much and not enough.

She whimpered his name.

"Come for me, Paisley."

She wrote romance. Had crafted countless love scenes. She'd always thought orgasm on command was a ridiculous fiction. But as he growled the order against her ear, his voice a rumble she felt all the way to her core, she shot up and over, crying out as her body clamped tight around his fingers.

He gave her no quarter. Before her walls had even ceased to flutter, he'd stripped off her panties and spread her on the bed. With molten eyes, he looked down the length of her body as he crawled toward her. His nostrils flared, a predator scenting his prey. It felt wicked and arousing and absolutely wonderful as he spread her wide and settled between her thighs. Lowering his mouth to her center, he laid waste to whatever was left of her, until she screamed through a second release that left her boneless and brainless.

When he stretched out over her, she had a moment to wonder when he'd gotten naked and donned a condom. But she stopped caring as his crown nudged her sensitive entrance.

Ty braced himself above her. "Okay?"

"I will be if you're inside me in the next three seconds."

He thrust into her in one hard stroke, and Paisley screamed.

Holding himself achingly still, he searched her face. "Did I hurt you?"

"No. No. God, don't stop."

Dropping his mouth to hers, he kissed her. She tasted her own release as he began to move, setting a steady, ruthless rhythm that shook the bed. She met him beat for beat as he plunged into her with a fevered desperation, as if hell itself were on his heels. As tension began to coil inside her once more, she wrapped her arms tighter, holding onto him with everything she had. On a roar, he broke apart, and the feel of his release had one more orgasm ripping up from her toes.

Ty collapsed on her, just managing to catch some of his weight on his forearms so as not to crush her. As delicious aftershocks rippled through her, she found enough energy to run her hands slowly over the slope of his shoulders, appreciating the up-close-and-personal feel of them draped all over her. When she could move again, she wanted to map them all with her tongue.

Smiling, she pressed a kiss to the side of his throat. "Yep, definitely better than we were at eighteen. And we were damned good then."

He made a noise and roused himself enough to peer down at her. "You look very smug."

Paisley stretched, squeezing her inner walls around his cock, still buried inside her. "Three orgasms and headboard banging sex seems worth some smug."

His fingers against her cheek were shockingly gentle. "You're okay?"

Because her throat wanted to close up at the tender touch, she forced a smile and continued stroking his back. "I'm pretty freaking fabulous."

He flashed a cocky grin that made her heart turn over in her chest. "I live to serve." Kissing her once more, he heaved himself off her to go take care of the condom.

When he came back, she'd burrowed under the covers and flipped them back in invitation. "Come back to bed."

One brow winged up. "You want me to stay?"

For one wild, reckless moment, she wanted to say yes. Instead, she patted the mattress beside her. "I told you I had no expectations beyond the night. But the night isn't over, and I'm nowhere near done with you."

He crawled in beside her, and there was no awkwardness. He simply pulled her against him as he had so many times before. Their bodies remembered what time and distance had dimmed. Paisley couldn't help but notice that his eyes looked less haunted and more like the boy she'd loved.

In the wake of stupendous sex, it was far too easy to wipe away all the years apart. To indulge in the fantasy that he wouldn't be walking away again. That this would be the start of something new between them. But for the life of her, she couldn't quite make herself let it go. If that made her a fool, she was the only one who'd suffer the consequences.

TY WOKE TANGLED WITH A WARM, naked woman. Paisley lay all but boneless against him, her hand over his heart, legs twined with his. His face was bent close to the riotous waves of her hair, as if he needed the comfort of her scent even in sleep. It was a helluva delicious scent, all mingled with his. The combination made him feel smug and possessive.

He'd stayed the night.

Did it even count? They'd barely slept, turning to each other again and again, until just before the thin rim of dawn began to peek through the window. Passing out from sheer exhaustion wasn't exactly a true choice. It was more like a nap.

But the truth was, he'd have chosen to stay anyway. He'd wanted to wake up with her like this. It was an indulgence they'd never had in high school, one he'd always craved. He had no business craving it now. No business indulging in anything when it came to Paisley Parish. But he couldn't find it in him to regret last night.

The dog scratched at the door, whining.

Paisley stretched and snuggled in closer, her breasts pressing against his chest and giving fresh inspiration to the morning wood that had been at half-mast. He trailed a hand down her back to curve around her lush ass. She wiggled against him, skating her own hand down his chest to curl around his dick. Ty groaned and thrust into her touch.

"Okay, so maybe there's a reason to be awake," she rasped.

Duke scratched again, whining.

"Maybe if we ignore him, he'll go away," Ty suggested. He could roll her over, be inside her in seconds.

Paisley moaned. "Whattimesit?"

He glanced at the clock, startled to realize it was far later than he'd thought. "Nearly eleven."

He'd actually *slept*. Dreamlessly. For the first time in longer than he could remember. No nightmares. No rocketing out of sleep, ready to fight. Before he could process the implications of that, Duke began to paw at the door in earnest.

"If this is what it's like to be a parent, I'm glad I skipped it," Paisley muttered.

Duke yipped.

She removed her hand and shoved up. "He's lucky he's cute. And we're lucky he doesn't have opposable thumbs. I don't think either of us wants seventy-five pounds of enthusiastic canine bouncing on the bed." Brushing a kiss to the underside of his jaw, she rolled away. "I'm going to go let him out, do the breakfast thing. I'll be right back to pick up where we left off."

She shrugged into a silk robe in some peachy pink color that diverted his brain to more interesting ways to begin the day than breakfast. Scrubbing both hands over his face, he watched her leave and settled back against the pillow, plotting exactly how he wanted to seduce her again. They could follow that up with a shower—together, of course. Then pancakes. Surely, she had the makings for those. And maybe there was a river walk somewhere in Nashville. They could take Duke and—

Ty froze.

Pancakes? Long walks with the dog? What the actual hell? He wasn't this domestic guy. This wasn't a relationship. They weren't just picking back up where they'd left off eighteen years ago. That was insanity. Half a fucking lifetime had passed since then. This was just nostalgia and natural chemistry combining into something explosive.

Really fucking explosive.

She'd rocked his world last night. And it had been...well, it had been more than he'd expected. More than either of them had been prepared for.

Then again, he'd never been prepared for Paisley. She'd always been the greatest surprise. Once upon a time, he'd been open to that. He'd believed she'd be his greatest adventure. For a long time, she had been. Loving her had been easy. Being with her had been a joy and a privilege. But that was before, when he'd had something to give her.

He wasn't that guy anymore. She deserved the world, not some broken-down soldier who'd left half of himself in a hellhole on the other side of the globe. He could and had faked it for a little while, but he couldn't do that long term. And he didn't want to see her face when she realized that he wasn't who she remembered. Didn't want to look into those big, brown eyes and see pity for the shell he'd become. Or worse, disappointment.

She hadn't asked him for more than the night. But if *he* was thinking like this, what was Paisley, with all her inherent romanticism, thinking in the light of day? She was a romance author. She'd always loved love. That absolutely hadn't changed in the last two decades. Sure, going into last night, she'd made the parameters clear, but what if she'd changed her mind? Could the girl he'd known, who'd wanted romance and marriage and forever, really have grown into a woman who didn't want those things, deep down?

He couldn't do more than this. Not even for her.

It was the temptation to try that pushed him out of bed. He knew his limitations. He understood better than anyone else what he was and wasn't capable of. The limits he'd set were for the protection of others as much as himself. He didn't want to hurt anybody, least of all a woman who'd once held his heart. There was no future here. No new start borne of a chance reconnection. He wasn't going to suddenly turn into a hero from one of her novels.

So, he needed to do what he hadn't been strong enough to do last night.

He had to walk away before he added her to his list of failures.

THE MOMENT the back door opened, Duke rocketed out, making a lap around the perimeter of the yard before sniffing out the perfect spot to do his business. Paisley hugged herself against the chill. Her whole body felt deliciously loose and used. So very well used.

Ty had stayed.

In truth, she hadn't quite expected that he would, which was why she'd embraced her inner sex goddess and kept him busy as long as physically possible. He'd been as insatiable as she, but Paisley couldn't quite shake the idea that he'd been running from something in her bed last night. He'd lost himself in her. Not that she was complaining. He'd learned a thing or three since he was eighteen. This growly, dominant version of him was totally working for her. She'd need to soak for a week if she expected to walk properly, but that would be after another orgasm or three. If she was being greedy, who could blame her? He'd grown up hot AF and knew what to do with it.

Duke raced back inside, turning circles of joy until she placed his bowl of kibble in the stand. He dove in, bolting down the food without even chewing. He'd be finished before she got back to the bedroom, but she could hurry fast enough to shut the door. She'd make up for ignoring him later. Mama had a sexy man in her bed, and she intended to make use of him again. Maybe she could convince Ty to stay another day. A full twenty-four hours of debauchery sounded like a magnificent use of a weekend.

Pleased by the prospect, she pushed into the room. "I was thinking—"

Ty was half-dressed when she walked inside.

Her nascent plans died a swift death, and she tried not to let the disappointment show. This was what he'd signed on for. One night. He'd given her what she'd asked. But it still stung to see him buttoning his tux shirt, obviously getting ready to go.

"Leaving so soon?"

He started pulling on his shoes, those nimble fingers tying the laces with quick efficiency. "I need to be getting back."

Retreat.

There was no other word for this.

What had happened between the sleepy, naked Ty she'd left in her bed ready for another round and now? Maybe he'd gotten some kind of call about something back home?

"Is everything okay?"

"It's fine. I just need to get going." His words were businesslike, matter-of-fact, as if they hadn't just spent the last twelve hours exploring every intimate inch of each other.

No sparing of her feelings then. The feelings she wasn't supposed to have caught during this little interlude. And she hadn't. It was just nostalgia and orgasms talking.

Paisley crossed her arms and tried to keep her tone light. "At the risk of sounding like a broken record, I'm not looking for anything serious here, Ty. You don't have to run off."

He rose to his feet with that silent, fluid grace his training had instilled. Paisley wished she didn't find it so sexy.

"I'm not running anywhere. And you said that

before. Why is that? I've never known anybody more serious about relationships than you."

That had been true once.

She shrugged. "That girl was a long time ago. After my second divorce, I decided that serious and I don't work. My expectations were consistently out of line with reality." Her ex-husbands had made that abundantly clear, and she hadn't been willing to lower her standards for a long-term partner. "So, I learned to keep things light and fun and short term. That works for me."

It tasted like a lie, one she'd been living by for a long time. But what else could she tell him when he was poised to walk out her door? The idea of letting him walk out of her life again had something akin to panic fluttering beneath her breastbone. It wasn't just about the sex. She'd missed *him*. But she had a feeling that saying so would just make him run faster.

Because this felt like the only opening she'd get, she strolled over to him, keeping her tone casual and flirty. "I'd love to pursue that short term with you." Not above using feminine wiles to woo him to her way of thinking, she trailed her fingers down his arm. "I think we'd both find it mutually beneficial."

Ty hesitated. She knew he wasn't unaffected by

her, knew he was battling his own lust, and prayed he'd lose.

"I don't live here, Pais. I'm in Eden's Ridge."

At four hours, that wasn't too far to drive from time to time. It might not be what she wanted, deep down, but she could work with that. "Perfect. Then we aren't in each other's back pockets worried about expectations. Just fun, when it works for both of us." She'd had this conversation, this arrangement, before and it had never left her feeling hollow. But it had never been with Ty.

He turned her to face him, skimming his hands down her arms before pulling her in and lowering his mouth to hers. Without a word, she recognized his goodbye in the lingering play of his lips. The heartbreaking taste of it flooded her, making her want to weep. But she didn't hold on and didn't say anything as he pulled back.

"Last night was amazing. I'm glad we ran into each other."

She understood that this was all she was going to get. Even as her foolish, nostalgic heart cracked again, she forced a smile. "Me, too."

"I've gotta get on. I'm already late checking out of my AirBnB."

"Sure. Of course." She wanted to ask for his number. His email. Something that wouldn't mean the absolute closing of the door between them. But she walked him to the door, with Duke prancing as escort.

Ty scrubbed Duke's ears and lifted his hand in a wave as he trotted down the front steps.

Despite the cold, Paisley stood on the porch, watching him stride to his truck. She'd known this was the likely outcome, even when she'd invited him home last night. It wasn't fair to be upset with him for sticking to the script.

He paused, one hand on the truck door. Paisley held her breath.

Look back. Look back at me.

Without turning, he called, "You remember that time our junior year, what you said when you were trying to talk me into breaking into the city pool for a midnight swim?"

Her heart began to trip. "If I remember correctly, it was something to the effect that you should lighten up, and you needed more fun in your life."

"You were right." Pivoting, he closed the distance between them, taking her mouth again in a frustrated kiss as his arms wrapped tight around her, like maybe he didn't want to let her go any more than she did.

Hope broke open inside her like the dawn, and

this time, Paisley held on. Maybe this wasn't goodbye after all.

As Duke began to bark—in approval or annoyance—Ty broke the kiss, resting his temple to hers. "Let's keep in touch."

They weren't quite the words she'd wanted to hear, but they were more than she'd expected. "I'd like that." She gave him her number, peering over his shoulder to make sure he entered it correctly into his phone.

Typing out a quick text, he pocketed the phone and offered an apologetic smile. "I really do have to go now."

Feeling buoyant, Paisley waved him away. "Go, do the thing. We'll talk soon." It was easier to watch him slide into his truck now, knowing it was true.

She stood on the porch in her flimsy robe, not feeling the cold at all as he backed out and drove away. There was no way to know how this would turn out. It might just lead to a few weeks or months of stupendous sex. Or it might be the opportunity she'd been waiting for since she was eighteen years old to show him their story wasn't over. Not by a long shot.

∾

I HOPE you enjoyed meeting Ty and Paisley! Their story continues in MADE FOR LOVING YOU, the final book in the *Rescue My Heart* trilogy. Or you can go back to the beginning to check out Ivy and Harrison's story in BABY, IT'S COLD OUTSIDE (*Rescue My Heart* Book 1) and Laurel and Sebastian in WHAT I LIKE ABOUT YOU (*Rescue My Heart* Book 2). Or you can hop on over to read about Emerson and Caleb in LET IT BE ME (*Men of the Misfit Inn* Book 1), or Maggie and Porter in BRING IT ON HOME (*The Misfit Inn* Book 4).

MADE FOR LOVING YOU

1

"Can you see my baby bump?"

Paisley Parish dutifully looked as her best friend turned sideways and smoothed her sweater over her rounded midsection. "Yes. Although, to be fair, you've been showing for a month."

Emerson grimaced. "I've looked *fat* for a month. I'm trying to figure out if I look pregnant."

Smirking, Paisley sipped at a mug of tea. "I mean, the regular announcements to all and sundry by your very hot, younger husband kinda took care of that for you." She'd never seen anybody more excited to be a father than Caleb Romero. His enthusiasm and absolute devotion to her friend was the stuff of romance novels. Paisley would know, as she wrote them for a living. The whole thing did her heart good.

Emerson rolled her eyes, but adoration was clear in the gesture. "He's so very proud of his virility."

"And you're crying so hard about everyone knowing that sexy, unicorn of a firefighter is yours."

Color pinked Emerson's cheeks as she offered a sheepish grin. "I mean... you've seen him."

"I have indeed," Paisley grinned back. "And if he hadn't been in love with you all this time, I'd have pursued him myself. Alas, he only ever had eyes for you."

Watching Emerson and Caleb dance around each other for years had been like the longest running will-they-won't-they romance plot in a favorite TV series. But unlike a show, Paisley had the option to call the protagonists out when they were being idiots. As a devout romance lover, she prided herself on intervening only when absolutely necessary—which she had when Emerson had lost her damned mind, letting fear get the best of her and walking away from the best thing to ever happen to her. They'd toasted Paisley at their wedding, and she was angling to have Baby Romero named after her in tribute. If her own love life was a hot mess, at least *someone* she loved was getting a happily ever after.

Emerson slid onto the other barstool at her kitchen counter with her own mug of tea. "Speaking of love and romance, how was Ivy and Harrison's wedding?"

And that just turned Paisley's mind to the precise hot mess she was trying valiantly not to obsess over. She'd recently attended the wedding of another writer friend and had her world turned upside down.

"The wedding was beautiful."

"You say that like the reception was not. Did something happen?"

She'd been sitting on this for nearly two weeks, and the not talking about it wasn't helping. Might as well come clean. "You could say that." She fixed her gaze on the contents of her mug, as if the chamomile held some kind of answers. "Ty was one of the groomsmen."

The thunk of Emerson's mug on the counter made her wince. "Ty? Like *the* Ty? *Your* Ty? The high school boyfriend, who smashed your heart to bits? That Ty?"

Paisley held in a wince. That was the part she'd been trying not to think about. "That would be the one."

After a long moment, Emerson picked up her tea again. "Wow. How was that?"

"It was fine." *Oh, brilliant, Parish. Fine. This is why you get paid the big bucks. You have such a command with descriptive words.*

"Fine like you were civil to each other at the buffet table? Fine like he got bald and fat and you're relieved you dodged that bullet?"

Paisley pressed her lips together. Damn, that tea sure looked interesting. Maybe if she stared hard enough, she could read her own fortune.

"Pais...spill." Emerson pulled out the Mom tone she'd perfected on her teenager, Fiona.

"Okay, okay." Maybe if she said it fast, like ripping off a bandage. "Fine like he grew up hot as hell, and we still have enough chemistry to light up metro Nashville, and I took him home with me."

Emerson's jaw dropped. "You cannot just drop a bomb like that and stop there. Details, woman!"

She shrugged with more nonchalance than she felt. "This Creeper of a guy was hitting on me, and Ty stepped in pretending to be my date."

"Wait...like he did when you met in high school?"

He'd done the exact same thing at a homecoming dance their sophomore year of high school, cementing his place as her first official hero. "It was a very déjà vu situation, except that he didn't hesitate when I kissed him this time."

No, where the boy had frozen when she'd laid one on him to sell the fiction he'd presented, the man had pulled her in and laid waste to her defenses with a kiss that had been playing on her highlight reel of the night. It was a helluva lengthy reel.

"Oh my god! It's like something out of one of your novels!"

It was, indeed. And that was part of the problem.

"What happened next?" Emerson demanded.

Eighteen years of wanting and wondering made me stupid.

"Creep went away, we danced, then walked down memory lane for a while, and I invited him home." She shrugged. "It wasn't a big deal."

One brow winged up. Damn, Emerson really had the Mom Stare down. "Do I look dumb enough to buy that? I know how bad he hurt you."

As Emerson had been the one to pick up the pieces when they'd met as roommates their freshman year of college, right after Ty had dumped Paisley and left for boot camp, she knew perhaps better than anyone how devastated

Paisley had been. And it was that more than any-thing else that had kept her from spilling her guts right after the wedding. She didn't want to answer the inevitable smart questions she hadn't been willing to ask herself.

"It was a long time ago." It was, and she should've been able to be as casual about it as she pretended to be. But when had anything with Ty Brooks ever been casual?

As the silence dragged out, confirming Paisley wasn't going to address that issue on her own, Emerson asked, "Was he as good as you re-membered?"

This Paisley could talk about. "No." She couldn't repress a purr. "He's even better." As he'd proved multiple times through the night she hadn't wanted to end. That highlight reel began to play again, cranking up her inner thermostat.

"So, what was this? Closure? Are you starting over with him? Picking back up where you left off?"

All excellent questions—none of which had answers.

Paisley shrugged again. "It was one fabulous night with no understanding or expectation of more."

Emerson's moue of disappointment echoed

her own. Not that Paisley wanted to acknowledge that outside the privacy of her own head.

"You're not even going to keep in touch?"

"He lives in Eden's Ridge now."

"It's a four-hour drive. Caleb and I have made it a few times to visit his sisters. That's not so bad."

"Not exactly easy dating distance." Even if he'd been so inclined. Which he hadn't.

"That didn't answer my question."

"We're keeping in touch," Paisley conceded. "But it's casual. Neither of us wants serious." *Liar liar, pants on fire.*

She'd done casual for years, since her second divorce had left her inherent sense of romanticism thoroughly dented, proving once and for all that men could be enjoyed but not counted on. It was all she could handle. So, she'd be fine doing casual with Ty, if that was all she could have. And if her stupid, foolish heart was aching for more, she'd get over it. Besides, she had more pressing things to worry about than when she was next going to get Ty Brooks into her bed, and that was a sad and depressing state of affairs.

Paisley's phone began to ring. *Joel Fisher* flashed across the screen.

Rookie mistake. Think about the problem, and that shit manifests.

Bracing herself, she hit answer. "Detective. Tell me you have something."

"DEPUTY BROOKS!"

Ty tried not to wince as Crystal Blue proclaimed his presence to the entirety of the lunch crowd at the diner. Not that there was anyone there who didn't already know who he was. Probably. Eden's Ridge and the rest of Stone County was a small town. He'd grown up in one much like it within spitting distance over the state line in Georgia, so he understood that, even at more than a year in residence, he was still news and still carried the mantle of New Guy. What he hadn't been prepared for was being considered fresh meat. The diner's cheerful proprietress seemed determined to matchmake him, despite all his protestations that he wasn't looking for a woman. Or a man. She'd run a few of those in his direction, too.

She had that gleam in her eyes as he approached the counter, and he abruptly wished he'd gotten takeout from Elvira's Tavern. Denver wouldn't try to marry him off with his patty melt.

"Crystal. Is my order ready? I've got some business down in Cummings." Why couldn't there be a convenient call from dispatch to back him up on that?

"Nearly. Have a seat, sugar." She gestured toward the lone empty spot of the counter, right next to a woman in a trim pencil skirt and blouse, head down as she worked on her phone.

He had a bad feeling as he slid onto the stool.

Crystal began to swipe at a nonexistent spot on the counter. "Have you met our Celeste?"

The woman looked up, dark eyes going wide as a deer in the headlights.

Ty could relate. "I don't believe so."

"Celeste is the head of our Chamber of Commerce."

He nodded to the woman, understanding he had to say *something*. "Ma'am."

Crystal beamed. "Don't these former military men have lovely manners?" Ty noted she didn't bother introducing *him*. It was understood that everyone knew who he was.

"Um, yeah. Hi." A faint flush rose beneath the tawny copper of her cheeks, and she flashed an awkward smile that told him she wasn't any more prepared for this ambush than he was.

"You two both love the patty melt on sourdough with curly fries," Crystal announced, preening as if she'd brokered world peace.

She was matchmaking by food preferences now?

As Ty tried to come up with a polite, noncommittal response, an arm slung around his shoulders. He recognized the weight and feel of it before the other man even began to speak. "Reckon you're too late, Crystal. Ty here was seen in the company of a mysterious brunette at Harrison and Ivy's wedding. Could be he's off the market."

Damn Sebastian.

Ty had been avoiding this for two weeks. It seemed his time was up. He turned a silent glare on the man who'd had his back on more missions than he could count. It was really too bad Ty was gonna have to kill him.

"Is that true?" Crystal vibrated with equal parts affront and interest.

Ty thought of the brunette in question, startled to realize how much he wanted to say yes. But what he had with Paisley wasn't a relationship. It was... Well, he didn't know what the hell it was. He wasn't willing to share with the class either way.

"My food, Crystal? I really need to go."

With a pout, she handed over the bag. Ty made as dignified a beeline for the exit as he could manage.

Sebastian followed him out the door. "So, who is she?"

The girl he'd once been willing to do anything for. Including letting her go when his life path would have broken her, no matter how much it had hurt him to do it.

"Just a wedding fling."

Even saying it made him want to wince. Paisley Parish wasn't *just* anything, but he wasn't opening up that vein with Sebastian.

"Well, whatever it is, we're all happy to see you get back out there. Garrett would be proud that you're starting to live again."

The familiar rush of shame and guilt swept over him, as it always did whenever anyone mentioned the best friend he'd failed to protect. Garrett would be anything but proud. He'd be lining up to kick Ty's ass for the casual, no strings arrangement he'd agreed to. Paisley was a forever girl, not a fling. When they'd both been preparing to go into the Army with an eye toward Special Forces, Garrett had called Ty a fool for breaking things off with Paisley instead of marrying her as Garrett had his own long-time girlfriend. From this side of it, with Garrett dead and Bethany a widow, it was hard not to think that, on this at least, he'd made the right call.

Ty didn't know if he was making the right call now, keeping in touch with Paisley. He hadn't planned to. Then again, nothing had gone according to his plan since he'd run into her at that wedding reception. He'd been riding on nostalgia and lust and the embers of other feelings he'd thought long dead and buried. His entire adult life had been spent running headlong into situations where others feared to tread, yet somehow this felt more dangerous.

After losing Garrett in the line of duty and separating from the Army, Ty wasn't in any shape for a relationship. He lived for the job now. It was the thing that had salvaged his sanity, if not his soul. That made him a shit bet for someone like her. All he had to give her was the physical. Knowing she deserved so much more than that, he'd tried to walk away from her. Again.

But Paisley hadn't asked for more than the physical. And when push came to shove, he hadn't been strong enough to do what he'd done at eighteen. He was enough of a selfish bastard to take her at her word because being with her was the first thing he'd done in two years that had made him feel anything but numbness or raging grief. Garrett would've been taking him to task for using her. Or advising him to call the damned preacher.

But Garrett wasn't here. There was, for now, only Sebastian, who was lounging against Ty's squad car, grinning.

Shit. How long had he been standing here thinking about Paisley?

"What?"

"Nothin'. I just think you're mooning an awful lot over something that's just a wedding fling." The grin got broader, taking on a Cheshire Cat cast at the prospect that another of their circle had been hit with the love stick.

"Don't be a dumbass. I'm not mooning."

"Sure, you're not." He clapped Ty on the shoulder. "So, when are you going to see her again?"

"What makes you think I'm going to see her again?"

"Because, until you got ambushed by Crystal in there, that was the most relaxed I've seen you in...hell, maybe a decade. Certainly, recent memory. Seems a shame not to repeat the experience."

Well, he wasn't wrong. And Ty would've been lying if he said he hadn't been thinking about her. Constantly. They'd been texting. He'd held himself back from calling her, as much to see if he could as to stick to the terms he'd agreed to. But he'd sooner be waterboarded than admit it to the asshat masquerading as his friend.

The radio at his shoulder crackled. "Deputy Brooks, this is dispatch."

Grunting, Ty dragged open the door to his Sheriff's Department cruiser and tossed in his food as he reached for the call button. "Dispatch, this is Brooks. Go ahead, Essie."

"We've got at situation down at 583 Westinghouse Road."

"What kind of situation?"

"Probable domestic dispute. Clyde is en route for backup."

"On my way."

Sebastian's smile had disappeared. "Be careful, brother."

"Always am." He slid into the driver's seat, nodding as Sebastian double tapped the hood in farewell.

Flipping on the light bar, he headed out to save the day.

2

Paisley knew the moment she laid eyes on Detective Joel Fisher that today was not going in her favor.

"You don't have good news."

Detective Fisher opened his mouth as if to protest, then spread his hands with an apologetic wince. "There's no way to trace the package."

She'd known that when she'd contacted him, having learned more than the average bear at the citizen's police academy she'd attended for book research eight months ago. Real life police departments didn't have the kind of forensic miracles so often shown on TV. But she hadn't known what else to do when she'd found the package waiting on her front porch.

"What do we do? It's escalating."

"Each contact has been non-threatening," he pointed out. "No actual laws have been broken."

She offered up an unladylike snort. "Please. Is that supposed to make me feel better? Let's call this what it is. I'm being stalked. Maybe taken on their own each gift doesn't seem like a big deal, but together?" Feeling a chill at the thought, she wrapped both arms around her torso. "They're getting more frequent, more personal, and more immediate to my physical proximity. It was bad enough when they were all going to my P.O. Box. That's why I have it. But this one came to *my house. This person knows where I live.*"

The very idea of it skeeved her out. She wasn't delusional enough to believe that her fans couldn't find her if they tried hard enough. But the idea that someone would try? That they might believe themselves entitled enough to invade her personal life? That unsettled her in a way nothing else ever had. It turned the profession she loved into something that dialed up her anxiety and made it hard to even write.

Joel tunneled one hand through his sandy hair, going gray at the sideburns. "I wish I could do more. But the sad, shitty truth is that, even if we knew who was behind this, none of it is an arrestable offense. Without an actual, verifiable threat, there's nothing we can do but document to create a case."

"So, I'm just supposed to wait until this whack job graduates to showing up in person and traps me in some kind of *Misery* scenario?"

To his credit, the detective didn't even blink at her outburst. "I understand you're unnerved. But so far there have been no demands, no threats. There's no reason to think it would go so far as to put you in any physical danger."

"Right, because my peace of mind doesn't matter at all." Paisley pinched the bridge of her nose. This was un-fucking-believable. Someone was engaging in a type of psychological torture, and the good guys could do exactly nothing about it.

"Miss Parish... Paisley—" Reaching out a tentative hand, he laid it on her shoulder. "—I swear to you, I am not dismissing your concerns. I've added this incident to the file with all the others. I'm doing the best I can with what I've got to work with."

The assurance made her feel like a jerk, even as it wasn't anywhere near enough. This man had been kind enough to endure her endless questions in the name of book research, even before the harassment started. He deserved more than a little credit for his patience.

She squeezed his hand in thanks for the support he'd so willingly offered. "I know you are. And I know that with a caseload of other, more serious crimes, this is nothing. I just…" There was no point in rehashing her frustration.

"I know." He squeezed her shoulder and released her, hesitating. "Listen, do you want me to come by? I can make some recommendations for your security system. You do have one, right?"

"Of course. And that's sweet of you, Joel, but not necessary. I'm covered."

"I'll at least arrange to bump up patrols in your area. Maybe a more regular presence of black and whites will help deter anything else."

It was better than nothing. "Thank you. I appreciate it."

Joel lifted a box off his desk. *The* box. "You want to take it home?"

She didn't. But she'd kept all the other ones as some kind of evidence, even though having it all in the house made her uneasy.

Gingerly taking the package, she rose. "I should get out of your hair. You've got more important things to do."

"Making you feel safe isn't a trivial thing."

"I appreciate you saying so." He could just as easily have been annoyed with her or called her hysterical. Plenty of other men would have gaslit her about there being a problem at all, but Joel had taken her seriously from the first.

"You'll forgive me if I hope not to see you again anytime soon."

He flashed a smile. "At least in my professional capacity."

It wasn't the first allusion he'd made to wanting to see her socially. He'd straight up asked her out after the citizen's police academy. But she hadn't been available then and now...now there was Ty. Sort of. So, she just smiled a little and gave a tiny wave. "Bye, Joel."

"I'll walk you out."

Before she could say that wasn't necessary, the phone on his desk began to blare. He held up a finger. "Fisher. Yeah. Yeah. Uh-huh." Reaching for a notepad, he began to scribble.

As his eyes flicked back to her, filled with apology, she wiggled her fingers and pointed toward the door. There was no reason for an escort to her car. She wasn't so far gone she didn't feel safe in the parking lot of the police station, and she didn't want to give him any false hope on the dating front. Their relationship needed to stay professional, maybe with a side of sort of friends. She never knew when she might need to pick his brain for more book research.

On the drive home, she kept glancing at the box in her passenger seat. This damned thing had ruined what was possibly the best weekend of her life. She should have been able to bask in the afterglow of magnificent sex and multiple orgasms. But no. She had to worry about this *person,* who didn't appear to understand boundaries and thought it was fun to rattle her.

As she strode up her front walk, the box under her arm, she wondered if that's what it was. Was it malicious? Could it be a case of someone with no social skills, who didn't understand how freaking creepy this whole thing was?

The sight of another box placed neatly in the dead center of her doormat had her going cold.

"Damn it."

Scared, furious, Paisley marched up the steps. She jammed the key into the lock and, swearing a blue streak, cast a hunting look around. Seeing nothing out of the ordinary, she scooped up the new package and hustled inside.

The moment the door shut, her adorable mess of a mutt was on her, joyfully barking hello and trying to climb her so he could lick her face.

"Okay, okay. Down, Duke."

She managed to dump her purse and both boxes on the entryway table so she could rub down her ecstatic pooch. He immediately rolled to his back, giving her his long stretch of belly for attention. Well accustomed to this routine, she scrubbed him from head to tail.

"Want a cookie?"

Duke leapt up.

"Let's go get a cookie."

The dog scrambled ahead of her, his paws slipping and sliding on the hardwood floor as he raced for the kitchen and the treat bucket. She snagged the new package and carried it with her.

Duke inhaled the peanut butter biscuit before finally flopping down to stare up at her in adoration, baseball bat of a tail sweeping the floor. She'd be able to actually do something now.

Studying the latest arrival, she took in the brown paper wrapping. Exactly as the one before. But unlike that one, this hadn't been shipped and dropped off by a delivery service. There was no address at all, just her name neatly printed on the top.

Someone had brought this in person. To her house.

Retrieving her phone, she snapped pictures

from all sides, just as she had of all the others. For a few seconds, she considered calling Joel to apprise him of the latest and ask if he could try to lift prints. But she knew there'd be none other than her own. She wasn't even sure brown paper would hold fingerprints.

Ripping the paper with perhaps more violence than necessary, she tore into the package. They'd found nothing special in any of the others. Why should this be any different?

Inside, nestled in plain white tissue paper, was a dog collar. With trembling hands, she lifted it out. Made of a bright red, woven nylon, the buckle-style collar was utterly innocuous. Digging into the tissue to see if there was anything else, she heard something thunk to the bottom of the box. Pulling out the tissue entirely, she found a metal tag in the bottom. She started to reach for it, then stopped herself to go retrieve a pair of tweezers. Lifting it out by the edge, she turned it over to read what was embossed in the metal: GEORDI.

Paisley's blood ran cold. Why would someone send her a collar with the name of the blind dog from one of her books? Was it a threat to Duke? She posted about him on social media all the time, so it stood to reason this person knew about him. And they'd been *to her house* to drop this off.

It wasn't an indictment by itself. But it felt too personal. If it had been a true fan gift of some kind, it would've been accompanied with a letter or note or *something*. Instead, it was just the collar, without even the usual card printed with *Your biggest fan*, leaving her to draw her own conclusions as to the message.

Paisley had a very, very vivid imagination, and her mind had extrapolated all kinds of horrors before her fingers even closed around her phone. Worried and a little sick, she scrolled to the right contact and hit dial.

EXHAUSTION AND IRRITATION dogged Ty as he stopped at the head of his driveway to grab the mail. Darkness had fallen, and the cold chill of winter in east Tennessee nipped at the exposed skin of his face and hands. It was nothing compared to the winters in Afghanistan and some of the other hellholes where he'd served.

Tossing the mail onto the front seat, he continued down the gravel drive, parking the cruiser next to his truck in front of the tiny cabin he called home. In the normal course of things, the place was one of his friend Porter's vacation rentals.

He'd offered it up when Ty had taken the job as Stone County deputy. Grateful to have one less decision to make, Ty had jumped at the offer. He'd meant it to be temporary, until he'd settled into the job, proved he could hack it as a civilian. Somehow, he'd never left.

He liked the solitude of living this far out from town, more than a mile from the nearest neighbor. And really, he didn't need more than the open-plan living space with a sleeping loft. It was just him. He had nobody to impress. But a vague, nagging sense of disappointment trailed him through the cabin as he went through the motions of starting a fire in the wood stove and stripped out of his uniform in favor of jeans and a flannel shirt.

Pausing behind the sofa, he glanced around.

The place felt empty. There was nothing of him here. No pictures, no signs of hobbies or interests. If he packed up his clothes and the collection of books, it would be ready for the next vacationers to walk through the door. No sign that he'd ever been here.

When had that started to bug him?

Grabbing a beer, he sank down on the sofa and began going through the mail. The usual smattering of bills and junk. And a thick, cream-colored envelope. The Georgia postmark had concrete setting up in his gut. Nothing good could come from home. He slid a finger under the flap of the envelope. The cardstock inside was heavy, like a wedding invitation. But this definitely wasn't for a wedding.

You are cordially invited to a celebration of life for Garrett Michael Reeves.

The date next month blurred before Ty's eyes as the invitation fell from his fingers.

Garrett's birthday. Bethany wanted to have a celebration of his life on his birthday.

How could Ty possibly celebrate his best friend's life when all he could feel was the gaping hole he'd left behind with his death? Hell, he hadn't even been able to look Bethany in the face since the funeral. He had, in fact, bolted from the wake after they'd put Garrett in the ground because he couldn't live with the guilt. How could she even think to invite him when it was his fault her husband was dead?

Snatching the card up, he exploded off the sofa and stalked over to the corner kitchen. With more violence than necessary, he stomped on the lever to open the garbage can. But he couldn't seem to make his fingers release to drop the card into the trash. Instead, he let the can fall shut and shoved the invitation into a cabinet. Out of sight.

It wouldn't be out of mind.

Prowling back to the sofa, he took a long pull on his beer and waited for his hands to stop shaking.

When his phone rang, he nearly let it go to voicemail. But one glance at the screen had his heart lifting.

"Paisley." He hoped his voice sounded smooth and cool instead of raspy with the tears he wasn't about to acknowledge. He took another pull on his beer to wash the frog from his throat.

"Hey, Galahad."

With that one greeting, he felt the stress and the years fall away, sending him back to a time when his only worry in life was when he'd get another smile, another kiss—and more—from this woman. She was a lifeline in a storm he was still learning how to navigate.

"That brings back memories."

"Naked ones?" she teased.

He let out a low chuckle. "Among others." But, of course, now he was thinking about the more recent naked memories and going hard.

"Is this the part where I ask what you're wearing?"

Amused, aroused, he sank back on the sofa.

"As I recall, you had a particular fondness for gray sweatpants and my varsity t-shirt."

She purred. "I always did love talking you out of them."

"You never had to work very hard for that." His favorite place to be had been at her mercy. "Is that why you called? To talk me out of my jeans and have your remote, wicked way with me?"

Five minutes ago, sex was the last thing on his mind, but the sound of her voice all but stroked the shell of his ear and down the side of his neck. He shivered, imagining her fingers trailing there and lower. His own fingers flexed as he thought about fisting his cock while she whispered dirty things into his ear. What would he want her to do in return?

"No, actually. I was hoping for something a little more hands-on." As appealing as that suggestion was, something in her flirty tone was off.

Fighting his own biology, Ty struggled to get his remaining brain cells to function. "You okay?

"Yeah, I'm fine. I was just hoping you might be up for company and some of that fun we talked about this weekend."

He wasn't at all sure she was fine, but the prospect of having her naked in his bed for more than a single night was enough to have his whole mood turning around. "Hell yeah."

"You're sure? I'll have Duke. He's got some issues with boarding, so I rarely travel without him. Is that okay?"

He'd met her cheerful disaster of a dog when he'd gone home with her after the wedding. It had made him consider whether he ought to get his own pup before he reminded himself of the long-ass days he put in on the job. "Sure. You know I love dogs. Bring him along."

She exhaled in clear relief. "Looking forward to it. We can both use a change of scenery." There was that off tone again.

Had she been anxious about asking him? They were still feeling their way around what the hell this casual thing was, but surely that wasn't it. Paisley was too confident a woman for that. No, he thought it was something else and wondered what was going on with her. Was that even any of his business under the parameters of casual?

No matter. He'd pry it out of her with orgasms. And if he didn't, well she'd be a helluva lot less stressed when she went home.

Already grinning, he said, "See you tomorrow."

3

Paisley's dreams were plagued with furtive shadows that had her tossing most of the night. She was uncharacteristically up with the sun, retreating to her office to try to work. Deadlines waited for no stalker. But between anxiety over what she might find next and anticipation of seeing Ty, her focus was shot.

She *hated* this. Hated that this person had distracted her enough she couldn't lose herself in the worlds she built. Hated that she was nervous in her own house. Hated that, in the wee hours of the night, she'd spent some time scrolling through real estate listings and considered moving.

She loved her little bungalow, damn it! It was *hers.* She'd bought it outright with her royalties after divorce number two—a major point of pride and mark of her success. The idea that someone had ruined her personal haven made her physically ill. Maybe she was overreacting. Maybe this was all just some awkward but well-intentioned person inadvertently messing with her head. But her gut said it wasn't, and she always trusted her gut.

Giving up on achieving anything productive, she loaded the car with her weekend bag, her laptop, and all Duke's considerable gear. She'd head out early, opt for the scenic route. If a tiny voice in the back of her mind said she was being paranoid by taking the long way around the city and doubling back several times before finally hitting I-40 East, she ignored it in favor of the latest Lucy Score audiobook she'd bought for the trip.

The stress began to fall away with every mile further from Nashville and every chapter of the grumpy, taciturn hero falling, despite his best intentions, for the sunshiny heroine. Nobody did that trope like Lucy. And if the story left her hoping for a similar reaction from her own grumpy hero, well, she had four hours to get that romanticism under control.

Despite the circuitous route and multiple stops to let Duke stretch his legs, she still hit Eden's

Ridge a couple of hours before Ty was due to get off work. She drove slowly through downtown. It was cute, comprised of a few streets of businesses, with cross streets leading to residential areas. She spotted a diner, a two-screen movie theater, and an adorable selection of shops with whimsical names like Moonbeams and Sweet Dreams. For a moment, she considered stopping to take a walking tour with Duke, but something made her keep driving on out of town. Ty had told her his place was a little hard to find. Better to drive on out and find it while there was still daylight, then come back to Eden's Ridge to take in whatever there was to see.

The world and most signs of civilization seemed to fall away as she followed the winding roads, navigating switchbacks and making her way up the mountain. Yeah, definitely a good plan to find this place in the daylight. In the backseat, Duke pressed his nose to the glass, panting with excitement as the trees rolled by.

When she spotted the right number on a mailbox at the top of a drive, she exhaled with relief. She'd turn around and find her way back to town. But as she pulled in, she saw Ty's truck and a sheriff's cruiser parked in front of the tidy little cabin. Was he home?

As if she'd summoned him with a thought, he

stepped out onto the porch in well-worn jeans and an untucked, plaid flannel shirt. His thick brown hair was rumpled, as if he'd been running his fingers through it. Her heart gave a simultaneous lift and lurch at the sight of him. Not because he looked good enough to eat, and not because of the impending orgasms. It wasn't even because the big bad Ranger turned cop could protect her from the nebulous threat of her stalker. No, her traitorous heart had only ever done this for *this* man. The first love who'd miraculously fallen back into her life.

That wasn't who they were to each other anymore. Hadn't been for half a lifetime. That kind of relationship was well outside the bounds of the fun, casual thing they'd agreed to. The parameters *she'd* set rather than see him walk away again. She'd take whatever he'd give her and be thankful. But as she slid out of the car, she was grateful for needing to deal with Duke because she didn't know the proper way to greet him. A smile and a wave? A hug? A kiss? She wasn't used to the uncertainty and didn't much care for it.

"I'm early. I didn't expect you to be home."

"Took the afternoon off."

To clean up his bachelor pad? Because he was

excited to see her? Pitter patter went her foolish heart.

Don't be an idiot.

Ty strode down the steps as she sprung Duke from his travel harness. With an ecstatic bark, the dog raced over to say hi before bounding away to pee and sniff.

"Will he stick close?"

Eyes on the dog instead of the man, Paisley scooped a hand through her hair. "Yeah." Great. Had she forgotten how to even *talk* to him?

"Good."

She barely had a chance to gasp as Ty slid both hands into her hair, tipping her face up and kissing her senseless. After one hard jolt, she melted against him, hands curling around those muscular forearms as he laid siege to her mouth. Every cell of her body pulled toward his and every thought emptied out of her head but the taste and feel of him and the answering clarion call of her own heart as every good intention to hold herself emotionally distant crumbled to absolute dust.

Paisley dimly registered a cheerful *Don't forget about me!* bark before Duke barreled into their legs.

Ty grunted, pulling her close to stabilize them

both, even as he used one hand to push down the dog. "Hi."

"Hi," she murmured.

He looked just as shell-shocked by the intensity of his greeting as she felt. At least it wasn't just her.

He cleared his throat. "We should bring in your stuff."

"Okay." She popped the trunk and grabbed her suitcase and laptop bag. "Everything else is Duke's."

Ty went brows up. "Aren't your kind supposed to travel like you won't see home for a month?"

Rolling her eyes at the patently sexist statement, she shouldered the computer case. "Not all women pack for the apocalypse. I don't need much. Duke, on the other hand, has a short attention span and does better when he's got lots of toys. I packed to keep him entertained while we entertain each other."

Those hazel eyes went dark. "Noted."

Paisley followed him into the cabin. She wasn't sure what she'd expected, but this wasn't it. It was small. Far smaller than she'd anticipated. A set of steep, narrow stairs that were more like a ladder led up to an open loft, where she could just make out a bed beyond the half-wall. The whole thing was one, big open room, except for what was probably a bathroom beneath the loft. A vaulted ceiling saved the place from feeling cramped, as did the windows everywhere that let in the light and the trees.

Ty tossed Duke's dog bed onto a spare swatch of floor near the wood stove and carried the bags of other stuff toward the kitchen occupying one corner. "Bathroom's through that door. Bedroom's up there. I'll haul up your suitcase when you're ready." Divesting himself of all Duke's accoutrements, he shoved his hands into his back pockets, an old tell that said he was more nervous than he wanted to let on. Somehow that made her relax a little.

"It's cozy." And it was, even if it was rather Spartan. She didn't see a lot of Ty here. The place was ruthlessly neat. Probably a holdover from his years in the Army. Was the lack of stuff a sign he hadn't gotten over the expectation that he had to be prepared to roll out for a mission at any moment? That had been his life as a Ranger for years. It was why he'd left her after high school, breaking her heart in one fell swoop rather than by degrees by trying to make it work.

They eyed each other from opposite sides of the couch. Maybe she should just lay one on him like she had at the wedding. If they got on to the naked portion of the weekend, they'd probably both be more comfortable. And she could relegate him back to the status of sexy boy toy. Maybe.

"Will Duke be okay on his own here for a couple hours?"

Paisley blinked away her visions of stripping Ty out of that shirt. "As long as I feed him first and hook him up with his toys. Why?"

"I thought we'd head into town for dinner. It's early enough yet you can get a little tour of the place before we hit up the tavern. You still like pizza?"

"Is the sky blue?"

He cracked a smile that left her feeling flustered and out of sorts. That smile had always made her a little stupid.

She hadn't expected to go out. In all honesty, she'd expected them to hole up and exhaust each other for the weekend. Dinner in town was...date-like. It felt like the kind of thing you did in a relationship. They'd both been very clear that wasn't what they were doing. But she was more than a little curious about what his normal life was like here, and she wasn't about to turn down the chance to spend more time with him—in or out of bed.

"WE CAN GET DINNER TO GO."

Ty pulled his attention back to Paisley, holding in a wince. He was being a lousy date. "What? No, it's fine."

One dark brow winged up. "Are you sure? Because you seem about as jumpy as a long-tailed cat in a room full of rocking chairs."

He hoped like hell that impression was more because she could read him than that he'd lost all ability to compartmentalize as a civilian. But she wasn't wrong. His instincts had been jangling since they got to town.

"Sorry I'm so distracted. It's just, we're being followed."

The blood drained out of her face and the fingers on her Yuengling bottle went bone white. "What?"

Alarmed at her reaction, Ty reached across the table to gently extract the beer and tangle his fingers with hers. "Hey, no. I'm sorry. I didn't mean to scare you. It's not like some kind of enemy operative. It's just a boatload of the town busybodies. Like Betsy Schoemaker back home."

Old Betsy Schoemaker had been a notorious snoop, who delighted in calling the cops on any couples who were fool enough to use the dirt road cutting through her heavily forested back forty as a lover's lane. He and Paisley had only made that mistake once, and they'd gotten away before the officer had arrived. But that hadn't stopped Lieutenant Petrie from stopping by to put the fear of God into Ty about the seriousness of trespassing and safe sex. To this day, Ty didn't know whether Betsy had some kind of wildlife camera on the road that had caught pictures of his truck or if she just camped out with field glasses and watched.

Paisley's breath gusted out and color returned to her cheeks. "Oh." Not bothering to pull her hand away, she reached for her beer with the other and tipped it back for a long swallow.

"What, exactly, were you imagining?"

"Don't mind me. Writer brain goes zero to ninety with little provocation."

Was it really her writer's brain on overdrive or did it have something to do with why she'd seemed just a little off since he talked to her last night?

She made a visible effort to relax, focusing those whiskey-gold eyes on him. "So, why exactly are the town gossips of Eden's Ridge following you?"

"Us. They're following us." He'd spotted the

first tail as he'd helped Paisley out of his truck a couple blocks down from Crystal's Diner. Jolene Lowrey, famed for her blue-ribbon-winning red velvet cake, had been coming out of Moonbeams and Sweet Dreams. She'd snapped a none-too-subtle photo of them with her phone and, shock of shocks, there'd been multiple faces pressed to the diner window as they'd strolled past. Reverend Hodgson's wife, Patty, was next, hanging back as he'd given Paisley the fifty-cent tour of downtown. She'd turned off abruptly into the hardware store when he caught her looking. Estelle Murchison hadn't even bothered trying for subtle. She'd just about gotten whiplash from watching them walk into the tavern.

"Us?" Paisley paused, considering. "I take it Eden's Ridge is cut from the same cloth as Coopers Bend."

"Bingo." She'd always been quick to pick up on precisely what he meant.

"So, tongues are wagging already, wondering who I am and whether I've taken one of the town's most eligible bachelors off the market."

"It's a distinct possibility."

"That explains the death glare our waitress shot me when she thought I wasn't looking."

He'd missed that but wasn't surprised. Trish

Morgan hadn't been subtle in her interest this past year. "I don't know why they keep trying to match-make me."

She snorted. "You're single, gorgeous, and new in town."

He'd also been more than a little bit of a train wreck when he'd moved here. Not that he'd adver-tised that fact. With a lot of work, he'd moved past the worst of it, but he still wasn't what he'd con-sider good relationship material.

With a wry quirk of his lips, he picked up his own beer. "They're overlooking the rather salient point that I'm not interested."

"Psh. Since when does that stop a bunch of wannabe grandmas from trying to snare you for their daughters?"

"Grandmas?" Ty felt the blood drain from his own cheeks. Taking a firmer grip on Paisley's hand, he leaned forward and stared into her eyes. "Help me, Paisley Wan Kenobi, you're my only hope."

Her dimples flashed. "Does the big, bad Ranger need protection from a bunch of gossipy old biddies?"

"Damned straight. They're terrifying." He was man enough to admit it.

Her big, bawdy laughter rolled out, loosening

something in his chest. God, he hadn't realized how much he'd missed the sound of it all these years.

"Is that why we came out tonight? To try to put a stop to the matchmaking attempts?"

That hadn't been on his mind at all. He'd been busy trying to figure out how to act and wondering how the hell could they do this causal thing when they'd once been so much more. The idea of it didn't sit well with him, no matter what he'd agreed to when they'd reconnected in Nashville. Paisley deserved respect and decency and just... more. Even if he couldn't give her promises, he could do better than treating her like the insignificant wedding fling he'd led Sebastian to believe she was. Guilt over his prevarication had driven him to suggest dinner out.

And even though he'd just spotted Marilyn Kincaid, his boss's mom, and Essie Vaughn, the Sheriff's Department dispatcher, ensconced in a booth across the bar, he couldn't regret it. Whatever hell got dished up over the water cooler come Monday would be worth it. He couldn't remember the last time he'd been around someone who'd known him before he was broken, and he wasn't above admitting that the feeling was its own special drug.

"We came out because I wanted to spend time with you." It was the truth, but it skated well beyond the boundaries of the casual thing she'd asked for. Because he didn't want to make her balk, he lightened his tone. "And because you were always a fun date. You did promise to add more of that to my life."

"So I did." She leaned forward, eyes sultry, smile devilish. "In that case, let's give them something to talk about."

Before he could close the distance between them, someone clapped him on the shoulder.

Damn it.

"Well, if it isn't Miss Brunette from the wedding." Sebastian stuck his hand into the space between the kiss he'd interrupted. The jackass. "I'm Sebastian Donnelly, one of this one's Army buddies. And you are?"

After a moment's hesitation, she sat back in her seat, releasing Ty's hand. "Paisley Parish. You were one of the other groomsmen."

"I was, indeed." Sebastian seemed pleased she'd remembered him.

Not fighting the scowl, Ty glared at him. "What are you doing here?"

"Picking up takeout for dinner. Laurel had meetings in Knoxville today."

"Then I'm sure she'd appreciate you hurrying up with it."

"Oh, the kitchen's not quite done with our order. I've got a few minutes." Sebastian turned his attention back to Paisley, flashing the friendly smile that his fiancée seemed to find charming. "And where has our Ty been hiding you?"

Ty bristled. He wasn't hiding her. They were here, weren't they? But as Sebastian waited for her answer as if he had all the time in the world, Ty wished they'd stayed in.

"I live in Nashville." She flicked a questioning gaze to Ty, then back to Sebastian. "I'm a friend of Ivy's."

God love the woman for knowing he didn't want to get into their past. If Sebastian got a whiff of that, there'd be no getting rid of him.

"Ah. Since she's still on her honeymoon, I'm guessing you must be in town to check out the spa."

Smiling sweetly, she lifted her beer. "You must have failed interrogation tactics."

Ty managed to hold in the bark of laughter—barely. "Sebastian is recently engaged and falls into that category we were discussing earlier."

"Ah." Paisley offered a sage nod.

Already looking vaguely insulted, Sebastian

narrowed his eyes. "What's that supposed to mean?"

"Subtle you are not. Whatever's going on between me and Ty is between me and Ty, and you'll just have to wait until he's ready to tell you himself."

His mouth opened and closed a couple of times. "Well. That'll teach me."

"Hope springs eternal," Ty muttered.

A waitress swooped in with a to-go bag. "Here's your order, Sebastian."

The bastard actually looked disappointed. "Thanks, Staci." He reluctantly accepted the bag and turned back to their table. "Well, seems I've got food to deliver to my lady. Paisley, so nice to meet you. I hope to see you again sometime."

She nodded. "Nice to meet you, Sebastian."

With a significant look at Ty, he gave a nod and headed for the door.

Paisley sipped at her beer. "I get the feeling that was a problem."

"Not a problem." He didn't want her to think he was trying to keep her from his friends. "It just means I'm the one who'll be interrogated later. It's payback for what I dished out when he met Laurel. Besides, he saw us at the wedding, so it was only a matter of time. I trust Sebastian with my life. He's saved it often enough. But with the details of my love life...hell no. He gossips like an old woman."

She pursed her lips. "So, what I'm hearing is that it's to your benefit if I keep you occupied and unavailable for comment?"

The sparkle in her eye had his blood beginning to simmer. "I mean, I'm perfectly capable of telling him to fuck off, but I like your way better."

Paisley grinned up at Trish as she arrived with a tray on one shoulder. "Can we get our order boxed up to go?"

Damn, he was in serious danger of remembering all the reasons he'd been ass over teakettle in love with this woman all those years ago.

He lifted his own hand. "Check please."

4

Paisley felt the eyes on them as they left Elvira's Tavern. Curiosity. Jealousy. Nothing she hadn't faced before, but in light of recent events, they made her paranoid. She'd come to Eden's Ridge—to Ty—to escape all that for a little while. There was no reason to believe her stalker had followed her here. This was just typical small-town nosiness. But for those few moments when he'd said they were being followed, she'd been legitimately terrified that this was the escalation she'd been expecting. That was how much this *person* had upset her equilibrium. Something had to be done about it, but, for now, she was going to take a page out of Scarlett

O'Hara's book and think about it tomorrow. She had a sexy man to bed.

In defiance—and just because she wanted to—she slid her hand into Ty's back pocket, cupping his ass. It had always been superb. She caught the quirk of his mouth as his arm came around her shoulders, tucking her against his side. Easy. Comfortable. And so familiar, her throat wanted to ache. It was yet another flashback to high school and the uncomplicated adoration they'd shared. A dangerous proposition. Things weren't easy or uncomplicated with either of them now, and she couldn't afford to forget it.

Determined to get them back to the naked, fun portion of the weekend, Paisley settled her hand on his leg as he put the truck into gear.

Ty glanced over. "We're playing that game, huh?"

"If you remember the rules of this particular variation of chicken."

He slid his hand over her knee, his fingers curling around the inside of her thigh. "As if I'd forget."

"It's not quite as easy as it was in that old truck of yours with the bench seat."

His hand skated up an inch. "I think we'll manage."

It was a game of torture, a slow seduction of proximity. With every mile closer to his cabin, they crept their touches higher, with little swirls and strokes of fingers meant to arouse and tempt. Her breath grew ragged as he trailed a finger up her inner thigh. His hissed out as she skimmed the edge of his erection. By the time he turned into his driveway, she was wet and desperate and wishing she'd worn a skirt. He threw the truck into park and, with more speed and efficiency than she'd imagined possible, unhooked her seatbelt to haul her over the center console so she straddled him.

"How the hell did we used to hold out doing that all the time?"

Paisley nipped at his throat. "We didn't always. I distinctly remember us being stupid enough to get each other off while driving when we were teenagers."

Gripping her hips, he ground into her. "Lucky we didn't wreck."

"So lucky." Fusing her mouth with his, she began to rock.

They weren't nearly naked enough, but she didn't think that was going to stop a first orgasm from curling her toes right here in the cab of his truck.

Ty did, though, as his hands stilled her hips.

"Shit, slow down. I have no intention of reliving that particular memory from high school. Inside. In an actual bed." The thrum of order in his tone had her lady bits swooning.

They scrambled out of the truck, grabbing the pizza—miraculously still in its box on the floor—and stumbled up the porch steps and through the door, where they were both confronted with the reality of her cheerful pup determined to welcome them back from an eternity away. Whole body wriggling, Duke leapt up with a bark of sheer joy.

"Down!" Ty snapped.

The tone worked on Duke too as he plopped his butt to the floor, tail swish swish swishing.

Resigned that naked fun time would have to wait a bit, Paisley scrubbed a hand down her face. "Protect the pizza. I'll take him out."

It took longer than she wanted. Duke had to circle the perimeter of the entire cabin, sniffing every tree and bush before picking the right spot to do his business. Back inside, they had to have a spirited game of tug to work off some of his boundless energy. By then, her stomach was making a bid to remind her that whatever else the evening held, it wanted food, so she and Ty stood at the kitchen counter, scarfing cold pizza and staring at each other with bedroom eyes.

As he finished inhaling his second slice, his gaze slid up to the loft. "Is Duke going to interfere with things?"

"As in, will he try to climb the stairs or howl through the main event? I have no idea. I didn't realize there wouldn't be a regular door. But he's like a toddler. Distraction is key. I think so long as he's hooked up with one of his puzzle toys, we'll be okay. For a while, anyway."

"By all means, distract away."

Paisley filled up three of the puzzles. It was way more treats than he'd usually get, but desperate times. As she put them on the floor, Duke bounced from one to the next, overwhelmed by his choices.

"Hurry." She made a run for the stairs herself, pleased when Ty bracketed her in with his big, strong arms.

"Up we go."

He nipped at her ass as it came level with his mouth. She laughed and moved faster, all but throwing herself over the lip at the top. Her blood was sizzling, and she was desperate to strip him down and lose herself in the frantic, sweaty heat between them. With that in mind, she faced the ladder. But as Ty reached the top, he slowed, prowling toward her with a fierce expression of wanting in his eyes. The muscles between her thighs clenched. Oh yeah, that look was really working for her.

But there was something else as he slid his hands into her hair, searching her face. Looking for...what? An answering wanting? She had that and more, always, for this man.

She was prepared for explosive heat and the borderline rough desperation he'd shown her after the wedding. But she wasn't ready for the soft brush of his mouth or the tender stroke of his hands as he drew her in. Instinctively, she began to melt at the touch before she caught herself and pulled back. "Ty." Could he hear questions in that single syllable? *What is this? What are you doing?*

He only stared into her eyes, brushing the tumble of her hair back from her face. "Just let me." He laid his lips over hers again, drugging. Seducing. And it didn't matter that she didn't entirely understand what he wanted, what he was asking. She couldn't help but give in. She'd never been able to deny him anything.

Circling them toward the bed, he began to strip off her clothes with far more dexterity than he'd had at eighteen. Her heart beat slow and thick as he laid her back on the bed, following her down to cover her with that incredible, battle-honed body. When she would've reached for him, he kept her fingers laced with his and began a lazy journey down her torso, sipping here, suckling there, mapping every inch with his mouth and hands. Or maybe he followed a very old map, as he lingered at the crease where her thigh met her hip, a spot that had always driven her wild.

"Ty, what are you doing?"

"Enjoying you. I didn't take enough time for this last time."

After the wedding, he'd been busy driving her out of mind with orgasms, a fact she hadn't complained about in the slightest. It seemed he was determined to drive her crazy with patience this time, and Paisley wasn't at all sure she'd survive it.

Ty rubbed his bearded cheek against the sensitive skin of her inner thigh, and she whimpered, needing so much more.

"I had to learn incredible patience in the Rangers. Sometimes we'd have to wait hours, days even, for the right moment to execute an op." His tone was conversational, as if his mouth wasn't millimeters from the promised land.

"Your point?" Paisley gasped.

"There was a lot of downtime to think. I used to think about this." He nuzzled her center through her panties.

"Sex?" *God, please.*

"Sex with you. What it felt like. What you sounded like. How you tasted."

The idea of it had her going impossibly wetter, likely soaking the panel between her thighs. She couldn't think through the implications of his words, only focused on the fact that he'd thought of her, thought of this, at least as often as she had after they'd parted.

Ty began to work the underwear down. "My memory is pretty damned good." Tossing the scrap of fabric away, he finally, finally settled between her thighs, spreading her open for his hungry gaze. "But absolutely nothing is better than the real thing." And then he dove in and proved it, licking and sucking as if she were the best thing he'd ever tasted.

Desperately turned on, Paisley gripped his hair, soaking in the sight of his head buried between her legs and the sounds of pleasure he made as she rode his tongue until she was breathless and flying. Before she'd even ceased shuddering from the aftershocks, he moved up her body and took her mouth. The taste of her own release had tension coiling fresh.

She nipped his lip. "You aren't nearly naked enough."

"Yes ma'am."

By the time he'd stripped and come back to join her, she'd found enough muscle control to rise to her knees. "Your turn." She pressed a hand to his chest, intending to shove him back and taste those V grooves at his waist that she'd been fantasizing about since the wedding. He'd had an athlete's body at eighteen, but these were new.

"Later." He pinned her hand to his heart and toppled back, pulling her with him. "Right now I want to watch you ride me."

As if she could resist an invitation like that?

Taking the condom he offered, she rolled it on, loving the thick feel of him in her hand. Hers. For the weekend, at least, this—he—was hers.

Swinging a leg over his hips, she straddled him, torturing them both by rubbing her slick folds over his crown.

"Paisley." His eyes were a dark, thrilling warning.

"You said you wanted to enjoy me. Turnabout is fair play. And you did claim that magnificent patience."

"Maybe I was wrong." Gripping her hips, he bowed up to take one nipple into his mouth. The motion slid the first couple of inches of him inside her.

Swearing, she speared her hands into his hair, rolling her hips to the suckling of his mouth, taking a little more of him each time. When he reached up to knead her other breast, she groaned and gave in, taking the rest of him in one long, slow slide.

They both moaned. Nothing had ever felt more perfect than the way he stretched her, filled her. She'd spent years trying to find this again and failing. No one had ever fit her like him.

His fingers curled into her hips, encouraging her to move. She bowed back to take him even deeper and gave herself over to the long, slow climb.

"You look like a fucking goddess."

She felt like one as she watched his face—the pleasure, the fierceness. When he gritted his teeth, obviously trying to hold on, she dipped forward, capturing his mouth and squeezing her inner muscles to push him past the edge of control. She loved him just the other side of civilized. Loved him desperate. On a growl, his control snapped, and he thrust into her hard and fast, until the kick and jerk of his release pulled her right over behind him.

$\sim$

TY HAD CONDUCTED all kinds of covert, stealthy operations in his career. He'd been taught to move in silence, in and out without detection. If push came to shove, he could probably plan a successful heist. But he wasn't at all sure he could crack an egg without waking the woman he'd left sleeping in his bed.

Gently tapping it on the edge of the counter, he glanced up. No sound. No movement. They'd worn each other out since Friday. Maybe he could pull off this breakfast in bed thing after all.

Pulling his attention back to the egg, he looked for the crack. Nothing. How did they make it look so damned easy on those cooking shows? They'd probably say something obnoxious like, "It's all in the wrist." Which it probably was.

With plenty of furtive glances up, he managed to break the eggs and fish the shells out. As he added some milk and a splash of vanilla, he knew he was crossing some kind of a line. Breakfast in bed wasn't part of the Casual, No Strings Sex Handbook. But then, he'd been operating off-book all weekend. He couldn't seem to help himself when it came to Paisley.

All those years ago, he'd cut her out of his life, knowing he couldn't keep her light and still function in the dark and shadows as the job demanded. Knowing, too, that to try would have wiped out the internal sunshine he'd so loved basking in. No matter how much he'd loved her, how much he'd wanted her, he couldn't make himself hurt her like that.

She'd changed in the last two decades. They both had. But that light was still the same, and being around her was an intoxicating reminder that there was more to the world than darkness. She couldn't know how much he needed and appreciated that. So, he was paying her back in orgasms and—God willing—French toast. He didn't want to think about what it meant or where it might lead. He just wanted to enjoy her, as he'd said.

Duke watched with great interest from the dog bed Ty had dragged to the edge of the kitchen. He wanted to be included so badly, and this had seemed the best way to keep him chilled out and quiet. Ty tipped a hefty dose of cinnamon into the egg mixture and carefully whisked it. Still no movement from the loft. Pouring the mixture into a baking dish, he reached for the bread. At the crinkle of the wrapper, Duke sat up, tags jingling, ears perked.

Ty held a finger to his lips. "Shh."

The dog rose to his feet, tail swishing like a metronome.

Keeping his voice low, he pointed. "No."

Instead of coming after the bread, Duke pranced to the door, bouncing on his front paws, his claws clicking on the hardwood floors.

Ty glanced at the loft again.

Duke bounced and chuffed.

"We already took a walk." Why was he arguing with a dog? This was ridiculous.

"You did?"

Damn it.

Paisley peered down over the railing, her hair a riot of tumbled curls around her shoulders. She didn't look altogether conscious yet, judging from the vaguely confused, half-mast state of her eyes.

"I was trying to let you sleep. We haven't done a helluva lot of that this weekend."

Her lips curved in a feline smile that, as always, heated his blood. "I don't believe you've heard me complain."

No. Screaming. Begging. Laughing. Never complaining.

"I had planned on a lazy morning with breakfast in bed." He hadn't had a lazy morning of any variety in longer than he could remember, but she made him want to indulge.

Her gaze strayed to the kitchen. "Is that French toast?"

Shifting from foot to foot, Ty resisted the urge to rub at the heat in the back of his neck. "Yeah."

"Is there bacon?"

That had a smile tugging at his own lips. "There can be."

"Coffee?"

"I didn't dare start it while you were sleeping. But yeah."

She shimmied down the stairs faster than he expected—but maybe he was distracted by the tantalizing flash of bare legs.

"You, Sir Tyson The Thoughtful, are a god among men." She braced her hands at his shoulders and planted a smacking kiss on his lips. "I'm starving."

When she would have dropped to her feet and stepped away, he looped his arms around her, holding her in place.

"You're wearing my shirt." It hit her high on the thigh and afforded him a magnificent view of her cleavage where she'd left it unbuttoned.

Without an ounce of shame, she nodded. "I am. And I'll let you in on a secret: I'm probably not giving it back."

That idea was way too appealing. "Like my football jersey in high school?"

Her expression went comically blank. "I'll plead the fifth." Spinning away, she sashayed into the kitchen to the coffee pot.

He liked seeing the ease with which she moved around his kitchen, making herself at home, pulling out filters, grabbing the bag of beans from the freezer. She was always so at ease wherever she was. It was an enviable skill. He still felt out of place almost everywhere in the civilian world.

But not with her.

The coffeemaker began to burble, and Paisley opened the fridge, bending over to peer inside, presumably looking for bacon. Prowling over on silent feet, Ty wrapped his arms around her from behind. Her shriek of surprise turned to laughter as he nibbled at her neck.

"Grab the bacon. I'll start the French toast."

The easy domesticity of it struck him as he slid the first piece of bread into the hot skillet. He hadn't imagined he could do this. But they moved in sync, hip-to-hip, Paisley manning the bacon, pouring coffee for them both.

He found himself staring at her as she offered him a mug.

She arched a brow. "What?"

Before Ty could open his mouth and probably make a huge mistake, his phone began to ring. "Watch the toast?"

"I'm on it."

He snagged the phone off the charger, frowning when he saw the sheriff's name on the display. "Brooks."

"Sorry to interrupt your weekend off, but I'm calling everybody in. There's been an explosion in the south end of the county."

The switch into work mode was instant. Ty moved toward the stairs. "What do we know?"

By the time Xander had finished briefing him, Ty was dressed and shrugging into his duty belt. "I'm on my way."

In the kitchen, Paisley was flipping the last of the French toast onto a plate. She offered up a rueful smile. "You have to go to work."

He heaved a sigh. "Yeah."

"I'll get packed up and out of your way."

Plucking up a slice of French toast, he tossed it from hand to hand, as if that would help it cool faster. "You don't have to rush off. Take your time."

She shrugged. "I would've needed to get on the road in two or three hours anyway. It's fine."

Their time together had been counting down all weekend. Ending a few hours early shouldn't have been a big deal, but he found he didn't want the weekend to end.

"What if you stayed?" So much for not being stupid.

"What?"

He should have just stuffed his face with the toast and waved goodbye, but he was in it now. "I mean, you can theoretically work anywhere, right? Is there something you need to be getting back for?"

"No." She dragged the word out several syllables.

"Then you could stay a few more days. Get in over at the spa for some pampering." Maybe if it wasn't just for him, she wouldn't think it was weird.

Paisley studied him for a long time, dark eyes serious. "What is this, Ty?"

He didn't have a good answer. "I don't know. I just... don't want you to go yet." The admission left him feeling exposed and vulnerable. He kind of hated it and wished he could rewind the last few minutes and take it back.

But at last, she gave a slow nod. "Okay, I'll stay. If you're sure you're okay with it."

Cupping his free hand behind her nape, her

brushed her lips with his, resisting the urge to linger. "I'll see you when I get home."

Snatching another slice of toast and some bacon, he headed for the door.

"Ty?"

At the threshold he paused, looking back. "Yeah?"

"Be safe."

"Always."

Still feeling the warmth of her lips, he headed out to do his job.

5

As an engine cranked up outside, Paisley stood in the kitchen, barefoot, in Ty's shirt, lips still tingling from his kiss as her ears rang with "See you when I get home." Duke chuffed at the door. The coffeemaker burbled. On the counter behind her, the breakfast they'd made lay cooling. In the sudden silence, the doubts came creeping in like ghosts, sapping away the flirty, happy buoyancy that had carried her through the morning.

She wasn't ready to go home. Above and beyond the dread of what might be waiting for her, she hadn't wanted to leave Ty and the little bubble he'd created this weekend. But she'd been prepared for the inevitable departure. The moment he'd gotten that phone call, she'd been trying to stuff all the messy feelings back into a box so he wouldn't see how disappointed she was that they were losing their last few hours. Fake it 'til you make it at its finest.

She hadn't been prepared for him to ask her to stay.

The request had alarm bells sounding from the perimeter wall around her heart. Keeping things easy and casual with him was already so incredibly hard, even before they'd both been seduced by the nostalgia of the way they used to be. She wasn't under any delusions that they'd been doing anything else. They both kept reaching for the past, for the familiar. There was a comfort in it. It seemed they were both at a place where they needed comfort.

But it was a dangerous game to play. Where was the line between then and now? It should have been easy to see. Eighteen years should have been a stark divide. They'd been apart for so much longer than they'd been together. But it was hard to hold on to the pain of all that time and distance when faced with the living man. The man who'd admitted to thinking of her for years after they'd parted.

Once, he'd been her everything.

She had never been able to put away all the what ifs. Not really. It was why she'd begun writing romance in the first place, needing the comfort of that dream that he'd come back for her. Over and over, she'd played it out on a fictional screen. And then she'd written about the moving on. The letting go. Those books had healed her. But a small, probably stupid, part of her had never stopped hoping. Indulging that hope now was like playing Russian Roulette with her heart. He'd nearly destroyed her once. What were the odds he'd do anything else this time around?

Unwilling to face the contemplation of that uncaffeinated, Paisley willed herself into motion, pouring the coffee, plating up French toast and bacon. She grabbed extra for herself and Duke. In her world, no bacon was left behind. Munching on a piece, she began opening cabinets, searching for the maple syrup. Ah ha. Last upper cabinet by the fridge. As she retrieved the bottle, some kind of card fluttered to the floor.

Scooping it up, she glanced at the formal type. Another wedding invitation?

...celebration of life for Garrett Michael Reeves.

Oh.

Her heart gave a painful squeeze. Garrett Reeves was as much a part of her high school memories as Ty. The two had been friends from the cradle, and she remembered them cheerfully saying they'd be friends to the grave. Even on their way into the Army together, she didn't think it had occurred to them that the end could come so much sooner for one or both of them. She'd been gone from Coopers Bend for years, but even she'd heard about Garrett's death in combat. Ty had said nothing about it, and she hadn't asked because it would've been diving into the deep end. She didn't need to ask to know how he was doing. They'd been brothers in all but blood. Garrett's loss would have devastated him.

That this invitation was shoved away in a cabinet said it wasn't a thing he wanted to think about. It was a good reminder that this Ty had serious wounds she knew nothing about. No matter what happened, nostalgia wouldn't hide those wounds forever.

Was agreeing to stay a mistake?

Carrying the food to the table, she called the one person who'd be completely honest with her.

Emerson picked up on the third ring. "Hey!" She sounded breathless.

"Am I interrupting something?"

"No. Mooch just decided to scale the kitchen cabinets again. Caleb's got him. When are you getting home? He could do with a play date with Duke to work off the excess energy."

"About that."

Her tone immediately turned wary. "What?"

Buying herself some time, Paisley nibbled on bacon, breaking off a piece for Duke, who sat quivering with desperate hope by her chair. "Ty asked me to stay."

Emerson took a beat too long to answer. "For how long?"

"He didn't exactly specify." More with the bacon nibbling. "A few more days. He got called into work a bit ago."

"You said yes." It wasn't a question. And why should it be? Emerson had known her for years.

"Yeah."

"Is that a good idea?" How many times had she heard this question? How many times had the answer been yes? Not as often as Paisley would've liked.

"Honestly, probably not."

"But you're still staying."

"I said I would." She kept seeing his face, those few moments of unguarded hope before he began to close off again, thinking she'd say no. And the relief when she hadn't.

"Paisley," Emerson sighed. "Are the orgasms that good?"

A laugh burst out of her. "I mean, yeah, but that's not why. He's different. And he's not. We agreed to the casual, but he's not acting casual." She told Emerson about the date Friday night and the rest of the weekend they'd spent talking and laughing. It was easy to be with him, as long as neither of them thought about it too hard.

"Do you think he's working his way around to asking for a second chance?"

The million-dollar question.

"I don't know. I'm a romantic. Of course, I want to think that. But I don't know how much of that is just me seeing what I've always wanted to see." She got points for admitting she wasn't objective about this, right?

Emerson stayed quiet for long moments. "It took you years to get over him the first time."

"I know."

She wouldn't get over him this time. In truth, she wasn't sure that she ever really had. His loss had just become a pain she'd learned to live with. An ache that let her know she was still alive.

"We both know you're not actually calling for my opinion. You've already made up your mind."

"I guess I just needed to talk it through. Hear

the whole thing out loud. I don't know what he wants. I don't know if this is going to fizzle out. Maybe he'll decide he's tired of me. Or maybe we both just need some kind of proper closure and goodbye on our timeline instead of Uncle Sam's. But I don't think I can walk away. Not without giving this a chance. Because I'd always wonder, and I'm so tired of wondering."

"I hope it works out for you, Pais. I really do. But I'll load in a stockpile of ice cream just in case."

IT TOOK an hour and a half to find the site of the explosion. It took two hours more to track down the culprits. No actual laws had been broken—there was, sadly, no statute against being stupid—but by the time Xander had finished putting the fear of God into the idiots who'd thought it would be fun to blow up a major appliance, it was headed toward three.

As the door of the Sheriff's Department closed behind the Duffy brothers, Ty learned back against a desk. "You think they'll shape up?"

"Odds are no. And if they don't, one or both of them will land in jail or an early grave. I'm hoping a visit from Agent Slattery from the ATF tomorrow will sufficiently scare them into behaving. For a while at least."

"God willing. You need me for anything else?" Ty was ready to get home to Paisley. The knowledge that she'd be there, waiting for him, had been a constant warm hum in the back of his brain as he'd done his duty. He was assiduously avoiding any analysis of that fact.

"No. Get on out of here. Sorry for interrupting your weekend." The sheriff's lips quirked. "My mama said she saw you getting cozy with a very attractive brunette Friday night."

Of course, she had.

"Respectfully, I know you've already had confirmation from Essie, so I see no point in commenting. See you tomorrow."

Xander's laughter followed him out the door.

He ought to hit up Garden of Eden for some groceries before he headed home. His cabinets were getting pretty bare, and he felt compelled to offer Paisley more than the frozen dinners that were his fallback.

A text came in as he slid into his sheriff's cruiser, after buying more than he'd planned from the market. Expecting something from Paisley, he was grinning as he pulled out his phone.

The grin faded as he read the group text from Harrison.

911. Elvira's. ASAP.

Ty's former captain and close friend didn't make overdramatic and unnecessary pronouncements, which meant something big was going down. Knowing he wouldn't get any more information until he got there, Ty thumbed back an immediate reply.

En route.

His brain spun on the short drive, wondering why they were being convened. Harrison and Ivy had only just returned from their honeymoon today. Was it another combat death among their military brothers? Organizing a suicide watch for others who were stateside? In the not-distant-enough past, his friends had done that for him. It had been Harrison himself who'd prevented Ty from eating a bullet to stop the grief and the guilt he hadn't known how to live with, so whatever his friend needed, he was there.

Porter Ingram was climbing out of his truck as Ty arrived, and Sebastian whipped into a space a few moments later. They convened at the door.

"Any of y'all know what this is about?"

Expression grim, Sebastian tugged open the door. "No idea."

"I didn't know he was even back yet," Porter added.

Bracing himself, Ty followed his buddies inside. The sense of creeping dread only intensified as he spotted Harrison sitting at a table in the far corner, a beer in his hand at three in the afternoon. The greenish tinge to his face didn't improve as he caught sight of them.

Ty and Sebastian dropped into chairs on either side of him, with Porter across the table.

"What's wrong?" Ty demanded.

Harrison picked at the label on his bottle. "I have been through some squirrelly shit. You were there for a lot of it. You know. But I'm not ready for this."

"For what?" Porter braced his forearms on the table. "Did you and Ivy have a fight already?"

It hadn't occurred to Ty that the problem could be something with Harrison's new wife. As the only single one among them, Ty figured he'd do better to keep his mouth shut.

"No. No. We're great." Harrison scrubbed a hand over his face. "She's pregnant."

Sebastian's mouth split into a wide grin. "I *called it!* Pay up, y'all."

"Neither of us actually took that bet," Porter pointed out. "This is a helluva piece of good news to get right before Maggie and I head down to Mississippi. Congratulations."

Ty had no idea what to say to this announcement. He knew military life and law enforcement. The whole marriage and family thing was so far out of his wheelhouse, he might as well be jumping out of a plane without a parachute. But he couldn't just remain silent while Harrison sat there looking scared shitless.

"What does Ivy think about all this?"

Harrison took a pull on his beer. "I mean, she's kinda freaking out. So, I had to be all cool and collected and pretend like I'm not losing my shit. But I'm totally losing my shit. I'm not ready to be father!" The whites of his eyes showed in the dim light, and his hand fisted the longneck bottle like a lifeline.

Ty felt the corner of his mouth twitch. Now that he knew nobody's life was in danger, he was starting to recognize the humor in the situation. Not that Harrison would appreciate it. "Dude, you can navigate a HALO jump from thirty-five thousand feet. I think you can handle a kid."

He turned panicked eyes in Ty's direction. "But...but...*what if it's a girl?* I don't know the first thing about what to do with a girl."

Porter sat back in his chair, a sappy grin on his

face. "Love her, hug her often, and don't let her date until she's thirty. Easy. That's my plan."

As he'd just welcomed his own daughter to the world a few months before, he was certainly the most qualified to offer up advice.

"Do you and Ivy *want* kids?" Almost as soon as the question was out of his mouth, Ty wanted to pull it back. It was too late for that discussion. Ready or not, a baby was on the way.

"We'd talked about it in that far off, someday kind of way. But we've been enjoying being just us, you know? But...yeah, we do. I mean...that's the dream, right? When we were out there in one hell-hole after another. To someday come home to have a wife and family. This just moves up the timetable by...a lot."

Sebastian snorted. "I'm gonna really enjoy imagining you sweating your way through diaper duty."

"Your time is coming, pal," Porter promised. "When are you gonna marry Laurel?"

Sebastian leaned back in his chair. "I've got plans. But we've got to line some things up first before we can set a date. We just got word back on another of the grants we applied for. It's enough to build a bunkhouse, so we can expand to a proper residential equine therapy program and serve more people."

As the three of them continued to talk about the lives they were building with the women they loved, Ty stayed quiet. His friends deserved this kind of happiness. They'd been through hell, and now was their chance to follow better dreams. He lifted a hand to signal the waitress. Once she'd brought a beer for each of them, Ty raised his glass. "To Harrison's impending fatherhood and our latest competition."

"Competition?" Sebastian asked.

Ty clinked his bottle to theirs. "May the best uncle win."

"That's not the only thing we ought to be toasting," Sebastian insisted. "Our boy Ty is finally joining the land of the living. He was out Friday night on a *date*. I saw with my own two eyes that he was *smiling*."

"Oh, shut the hell up."

"Really? That's awesome, man. Who is she?" Harrison asked.

Sebastian continued as if Ty wasn't sitting right there. "I've been wanting to ask if you know her. Paisley Parish. She said she was a friend of Ivy's."

"Oh yeah, I've met her a couple times. Bold,

fun, and funny. Great laugh. I think she'll be good for you."

Ty never imagined himself being happy like the rest of them. He didn't deserve happy. So what the hell was he doing with Paisley? He wasn't the marriage and family guy. She hadn't asked for that, but he hadn't exactly been faithful to the casual spirit of the agreement she had asked for. What if, by indulging this...whatever it was, he was giving her expectations? That would be downright cruel, and she was the last person he'd ever want to hurt.

He'd asked her to stay.

Shit.

He'd made a huge mistake.

Needing to escape the happiness and the teasing and the attention, he shoved back from the table. "I gotta go. Congrats to you and Ivy."

"Oh now, come on, we were just joking," Sebastian protested.

Ty threw down some bills to cover the tab and shook his head. He needed to go do damage control.

6

She hadn't been looking for the book. She hadn't been deliberately poking around Ty's place at all beyond what was necessary to find a wooden bowl for the fruit that would ruin in that bag on top of the microwave or the basket she'd found for the pretty greenery and pinecones she'd gathered on her afternoon walk. And, okay, she'd needed the extra blankets she'd finally located in a chest because the wood stove had gone out and she didn't know how to relight it. But how was she to know his library, such as it was, would be in the cleverly concealed drawers beneath the sofa? And why shouldn't she have looked? She was an author, a reader. She loved books. He had several of Ivy's thrillers, some of Harrison's sci-fi, an assortment of fantasy she wasn't as familiar with. And many of hers.

He'd told her that weekend of the wedding that he'd read and liked her books. She'd been utterly mortified, not only because he was far from her target audience, but because she'd been writing thinly veiled versions of him all this time. Or the him she'd imagined he'd become. If he'd recognized himself, he hadn't called her out on it, and Paisley had let that detail go.

She remembered it now as she lifted the battered volume. The edges were stained, the pages wavy, as if it had gotten wet at some point. The cover was a little frayed and white around the corners, with a multitude of bends and folds, like maybe it had been shoved into a rucksack in a hurry. Maybe it had been. The spine was creased in the way of a favorite that had been visited again and again. Running a finger over her own name, she wondered why this one? There were a few others in the box, but none that had been this well read. It was one of her few romantic suspense novels, part of a series about a private security firm run by former military types. What was it about this story that had made him come back to it over and over? The redemption arc? The friends-to-lovers plot? Flipping pages, she let the book fall open. But before she could see what scene he'd reread, she heard a key in the lock.

Feeling guilty, she hurriedly put the book back and shoved the drawer back under the sofa, throwing herself back into the nest of blankets.

Ty came in laden with grocery bags. His gaze automatically swept the cabin, pausing on the fruit bowl she'd placed on the tiny butcher block island and the basket of greenery on the coffee table beside her laptop. The mouth that had already been frowning seemed to dip further.

"What's with the green stuff?"

"I picked it on my walk this afternoon. I thought it smelled nice."

On a grunt, he navigated around Duke to put the groceries down on the kitchen counter. When he began unloading food instead of kissing her hello or otherwise acknowledging her presence, Paisley knit her fingers together. There was a tension around his eyes and mouth and a stiffness in the set of his shoulders. Was he troubled about work? Whatever had happened must've been out of the ordinary, or he wouldn't have been called in with such haste. Or was it something else? She hated not knowing how to act, what to say.

He solved the issue by asking first. "Get any work done?"

"Some. I'm not used to this kind of quiet, with no traffic. Plenty of room to think."

He grunted again, still not looking at her. Something was definitely off. This was Now Ty, not her familiar Ty. Maybe this was the norm for him. She had no reason to believe that the fun, playful side she'd been coaxing out of him was more than a temporary thing. Something akin to vacation personality. How you behaved when you weren't in your real life. She was painfully aware she wasn't part of his real life. Flirting him out of this mood felt like the wrong move, but she didn't know the right one.

Duke pawed at the door. She rose to let him out. The shadows outside were growing long. The sun would be totally down soon. "Don't go far." Shutting the door behind him, she decided to take the plunge into the River Awkward. "How was work? Can I even ask about that?"

His shoulders jerked. "It's not classified. A couple of idiots decided it was a good idea to fill a chest freezer with Tannerite and shoot it."

"I don't know what that means, but I'm guessing it's bad?"

"Tannerite is what's known as a binary explosive target. It's used for long-range firearms practice. Basically, it's got two parts that, when mixed and hit with a high-velocity round, go boom."

She'd grown up in the small-town South, where there'd been plenty of good ol' boys who liked to hunt and play with guns. She could well imagine the kind of trouble this scenario might have caused. "Did anyone get hurt?"

Ty scrubbed a hand over his face. "By the grace of God, no. A copse of trees stopped the shrapnel from tearing them apart. They were damned lucky. There was a guy in Alabama last year who managed to blow his own leg off playing around with the stuff."

Paisley covered her mouth in horror. Was that why he seemed off? Did the explosives bring up bad memories? Make him think of Garrett? She didn't actually know the details about how Garrett had died. Now wasn't the time to ask.

"Were they arrested?"

"They scared the shit out of their neighbors for miles—shook the ground when it went off—but didn't actually break any laws. The sheriff hauled them in for a talking-to, and they'll be getting a visit from the ATF tomorrow."

She wasn't sure what to do. Comfort or retreat? Did he even need comfort? He'd barely even looked at her since he came in the door. It was so far from the warm kiss and "I'll see you when I get home" he'd left her with this morning, she felt cold.

Did he regret asking her to stay? She'd worried about it herself after he'd gone. It was completely understandable he might second-guess the impulse. And it *had* been an impulse—one born of the pleasure and the fun and the undeniable pull they still felt between them.

She craved a true second chance with him, but pushing too far, too fast would likely do more harm than good. Maybe she should give him an out. But what if he took it? What if this was her only shot? Disgusted with her lack of backbone, she decided to lead with her heart. If he rejected the overture, at least she'd know.

Crossing over, she wrapped her arms around him from behind, resting her cheek against his back, feeling the outline of his Kevlar vest. It covered the scars neither of them had acknowledged in all their intimate moments, but she was aware of them now, wondering exactly how deep they went. He went stock still, both hands braced on the counter.

Her heart tripped, but she just held on. She could acknowledge, to herself at least, that she'd always hold on to him. "I'm sorry you had a crap day."

After a long moment, his hand covered hers and the knots in her stomach loosened. But then his fingers were untangling hers, and he was stepping away.

Heart sinking, Paisley braced herself for the goodbye she didn't want.

TY STEPPED AWAY FROM HER, feeling wooden and hollow as he turned, determined to do the right thing. But when he met her eyes, he saw naked grief there before the shutters came down again. He was already hurting her without even trying. Calling himself ten kinds of asshole, he pulled her in, needing to offer some kind of comfort, even though he was the problem. Her hands curled in the front of his shirt, and he couldn't stop himself from burying his face in her hair. She smelled of warm vanilla and the sharp cedar of his body wash.

Paisley burrowed against him, holding tight. How could he send her away now? How could he put that look in her eyes again? He'd had nightmares about it for months after he'd shipped out.

He'd never, ever forgotten the sound of her tears when he'd broken things off.

You are a coward. You're weak. You're selfish.

He'd been none of those things at eighteen. But then, he'd only been a shell of himself since he'd left the Army. A ghost going through the motions. The only time he'd felt like he had any substance at all was when he was touching this woman.

He opened his mouth to apologize but what came out was, "Better now."

And it was. The feel of her grounded him, leeching away some of the tension he carried. He didn't know how to let that go, even though he should.

They stood like that for a long time, breathing each other in, until Duke scratched at the door. Pressing a kiss to her temple, Ty stepped back and went to let the dog in. "How do you feel about nachos for dinner?"

It was a helluva non sequitur, but they both needed some normal.

"Amenable." She poked in the bags. "You got the fixin's for fresh guac?"

"Of course."

Duke pranced in and gave a cheerful leap, trying to kiss Ty's face.

"Down." When his butt hit the floor, Ty obliged the mutt with a rub, noticing the bright red collar. "Do you change out his collar to accessorize or what?"

"Huh?"

"Duke's collar. It's different from this morning."

"I didn't..." As her gaze dropped to the dog, all the blood drained out of her face. She visibly shook as she rushed over.

The hair on Ty's arms stood up. "Pais?"

"No." The word came out in a tremulous whisper. Not directed at him. Her eyes were fixed on the collar, a dawning horror moving across her face. She lunged for Duke, fumbling to get the collar off. "No, no, no, no, no, no!"

"What's wrong?"

Her hands raced over the dog, searching for what? Injury? He seemed fine. No visible blood or wound, though he whined, clearly picking up on his mistress's distress.

"Paisley."

"He's here. He followed me."

Ty remembered her reaction to his assertion they were being followed at the tavern Friday night and went on high alert. "Who?"

"I don't know! But he's been in my house! This

collar was in a box, on a shelf in my closet, when I left to come here."

Which meant someone had broken in to take it and followed or tracked her here.

Ty straightened. "Stay here. Lock the door behind me."

He sprinted up the drive, but there were no vehicles on the winding road. Turning back to face the cabin, he studied the surrounding woods with sharp eyes. Was somebody watching, sticking around to see the reaction he'd inspired? He had questions, so many questions, as he circled around to the west side of the property, where he'd heard Duke barking. He didn't know exactly what he was looking for, and the light was going fast. The nearest road was on the other side of the next ridge. Unless their perpetrator had hiked a lot further afield, that was the most logical place to have parked.

Ty jogged through the woods, scanning for signs of passage and hoping like hell he wasn't destroying any evidence on the way. Finding nothing by the time he made it to the top of the ridge, he started to turn back. Whoever had been here was likely long gone.

The sound of a distant engine had him pivoting, scrambling down through the trees to get to the road below. But when he burst free of the trees, onto pavement, there was no one and nothing to see.

"Shit."

It was full dark when he made it back to the cabin. He unlocked the door, grateful he still had his keys on him. Paisley had retreated to the sofa, locking her arms around Duke, who sprawled across her lap, still trying to lick at the tears streaming down her chalk-white cheeks.

"Did you find anything?"

"No."

"We should call the vet. What if he did something horrible to Duke? Poisoned him or gave him pork bones or..." She trailed off, pressing her face to her dog's fur, her brain clearly still spinning with the possibilities.

Ty had seen almost every mood of this woman. Joy. Excitement. Annoyance. Anger. Upset. Arousal. But he'd never seen her truly afraid, ever. The sight of that fear etched into her face had every protective instinct he possessed roaring to life.

"Has he thrown up? Behavior changed? Anything?"

"No. But—"

There were a thousand terrors in that "but",

and Ty knew she'd never settle until she knew for sure. He pulled out his phone. "We don't actually have a vet in Eden's Ridge, but I've got a friend who can help."

Sebastian had more knowledge about animals than anybody else Ty knew. His specialty was horses, but at the moment, beggars couldn't be choosers, and Duke was probably fine. This was more about putting Paisley at ease. He sent a quick text with the essentials.

Sebastian's reply came back almost immediately. **On my way.** After a moment, the bubble popped back up, indicating he was typing another response. **Is this a just me situation or do we want the whole team?**

Hell if he knew. But by God, he was getting the full story out of her one way or the other. He tapped out an answer. **Still getting the details.**

Sebastian came back. **Understood. En route.**

"He'll be here as quick as he can." Crossing over, he sat on the edge of the coffee table, bracing his arms on his knees as he leaned toward her. "Why didn't you tell me you had a stalker?"

She cuddled closer to the dog. "I didn't think it would follow me. I came here to get away."

"For a naked distraction," he said flatly. He'd

been on board with that. So why did it feel like such an insult now?

Paisley winced. "Don't make it sound like that."

"Like what?"

"Like you were just some convenient warm body. I wanted to see you."

"But you didn't want to tell me about this." Didn't she trust him?

"It's not your problem. The police in Nashville are handling it, insofar as it can be handled. And until now nothing that happened could be classified as an actual crime."

Unless they could prove someone broke into her house back in Nashville, this didn't count as one either. But at least now he knew why she'd seemed off. It stuck in his craw that she hadn't confided in him. That he hadn't pushed harder to get at what was bothering her. He'd *sensed* something was wrong. If he'd known it was this, he would've... Well, he didn't know what he would have done. Not left her alone today, for one.

"How long has this been going on?"

"Months. Well before we ran into each other again."

He hadn't seen her in years before a few weeks ago. She hadn't been his to protect. Yet hearing that someone had been, at the very least, harassing her for months felt like another failure.

"I'm a cop, Paisley. I don't understand why you wouldn't just tell me about this to begin with. Maybe not after the wedding, but when you called to come up here. Something happened to prompt that, didn't it? Something that spooked you?" Rewinding their interactions, he could see it.

She just nodded, wordless.

"Did you think I'd dismiss you? Have the police in Nashville ignored you?"

"No. I..." Her throat worked as she seemed to search for words. "I didn't tell you because that's relationship stuff, and that's not what we agreed we were doing."

Everything in him rejected her explanation. "Oh, fuck that. It's friend stuff. Naked tango benefits or not, I'm still that, and I'm going to help you get to the bottom of this. What's the name of the detective in charge of the case?"

Surprise wiped away some of the fear. Jesus, did she think so little of him? But really, what did she have to base her opinion on? He'd agreed to this no strings bullshit. Why should she expect anything more?

Because it's me, damn it.

"Um, it's Joel Fisher. I've got his number in my

phone. He'll be more likely to answer if you call from mine." Loosening her grip on Duke, she entered the passcode and handed it over. The fact that she wasn't protesting his intervention told him plenty about how rattled she was.

The detective answered after two rings. "Paisley? Is everything okay?"

Ty didn't like the familiar use of her first name or the warm tone of concern in the other man's voice. "Detective Fisher, this is Deputy Ty Brooks with the Stone County Sheriff's Department. I'm here with Miss Parish. We have reason to believe that someone has broken into her house in Nashville. I need you to send a unit to check on things."

After a beat, Fisher responded with considerably less warmth. "I've had extra patrols in the area. Nothing's been reported, but, of course, I'll have them look more closely. Let me speak to Paisley."

Translation: I'm not doing squat until I confirm she's okay and you are who you say you are.

Approving of the man's caution, Ty handed over the phone.

"Hey, it's me. No, no, I'm...well, okay I'm not fine. But I'm safe." She paused, sighed. "There was another one on Thursday when I got home from the station. No address this time. Just dropped off on the front porch." Another pause. "We had literally just had a conversation about how there was nothing you could do. I didn't see the point in bothering you again the same day."

So, Ty wasn't the only one she hadn't felt like informing. Stubborn woman.

"Yeah, well, you've finally got something actionable. This one was a dog collar, which I left in a closet in the guest room when I left town. About half an hour ago, Duke came back in from doing his business wearing it. Someone's *been in my house*, Joel."

She was on a first name basis with the detective? Was that only because of this case or did she know him more personally? What did it matter if she did?

"No, I'm safe where I am for now. Deputy Brooks has me covered. But I would really appreciate it if you could send somebody to check on my house and call back to let us know what you find. Yeah. Yeah. Thank you. Do you need to talk to the Deputy again?"

Paisley offered him the phone.

"Detective."

"I don't know what she's told you about her situation, but whoever is harassing her just crossed a major line. There's not been anything up to this point that suggested an outright threat to her person, but I don't like this escalation. Do whatever's necessary to ensure her safety."

Regardless of the nature of their relationship, Ty appreciated the other man taking the situation seriously. A lot of cops wouldn't. His gaze slid back to Paisley. A little bit of color had come back into her cheeks. "You can be assured I will. Let us know what you find out."

7

"I think it's safe to say that this guy is just fine." As if to thank him for the diagnosis, Duke bounced up to give Sebastian a sloppy kiss.

Paisley released a slow breath, finally able to let go of one fear. "Thank you. I know it was probably an overreaction, but I just... He's my baby. If anything happened to him, I don't know what I'd do."

"Nonsense, of course you were worried," Laurel soothed, squeezing her shoulder. Sebastian's fiancée was a take-charge, no-nonsense sort of woman. Paisley didn't really know why she was here, but having another woman around was comforting. "He's a total sweetheart of a pup."

"I've always loved that he's never met a stranger. But now… Obviously, I need to keep a closer eye on him."

Sebastian scruffed Duke's ears, frowning. "Are you sure he didn't know whoever did this?"

That was an even more horrifying thought. That someone she knew might be behind all this. "I'm not sure of anything."

"We'll figure it out," Ty assured her. He'd been totally locked down since the conversation with Joel, but she could see the simmer of temper underneath in the leashed power of his body. He was pissed she'd kept him in the dark and pissed about the situation in general, but she had to admit to feeling better that he knew. She had no idea what he'd be able to do that Metro PD hadn't already tried, but he seemed so terrifyingly capable. Or maybe that was her inherent romanticism casting him in hero-colored glasses.

Another knock sounded.

Sebastian straightened. "Ah, that'll be the cavalry. I figured I'd go ahead and get them en route since you choose to live at the ass end of the county."

"The rest of who?" Paisley asked.

Ty opened the door, all calm, collected, and in control. "Thanks for coming."

Harrison and Ivy stepped inside.

"I didn't know you were back from your honeymoon!"

"Only just." As Harrison accepted Duke's enthusiastic greeting, Ivy came straight over and wrapped Paisley in a hug. "It's good to see you, girl. We didn't get to catch up at the wedding. But I guess you were sufficiently entertained." One corner of her mouth twitched, and she arched her brows in question.

"Something like that." She knew perfectly well there'd be a more overt demand for details later.

"Any word back from the detective?" Harrison asked.

She shifted her attention to Ty. "You already told them?"

"Only the essentials, which is all I know. You're about to tell us all of it." Without batting an eye, he turned back to Harrison. "To answer your question, the house was locked but there are scratches around the door where the lock was probably picked. Alarms didn't go off. I'll get both of those taken care of tomorrow when we get to Nashville and meet with Detective Fisher."

The men nodded, as if this made complete sense.

Paisley crossed her arms. "Excuse me?"

Ty shrugged. "There's no reason to go tonight. Metro PD has eyes on your house, and we already know whoever did it is likely closer to here than there."

She blinked, trying to process. "You're going back to Nashville with me?"

"Of course." His mouth pulled down, as if he was annoyed the thought hadn't occurred to her. "I want a look at things myself and to talk to Fisher about the case in person. And you need to get more clothes before we come back here."

"Come back here," she repeated, her head spinning.

"You're staying with me until this is resolved."

If Ty noticed the others' startled reactions to his announcement, he didn't show it. He didn't even seem to be aware of her rising level of annoyance.

"I'm what now?"

"It makes the most sense. You can work anywhere, and I can protect you better here. My town. My turf."

She waited to see if he'd add his woman. But of course, he didn't. He was too busy orchestrating her life like some kind of op, as if she were a chess piece on a board instead of a person with wants, desires, and opinions of her own.

"I didn't ask you for any of this." Considering there was a potent blend of temper and anxiety kicking through her, Paisley thought she kept her tone admirably even.

"Yeah. And we'll talk about that later."

A headache started to claw its way up the back of her neck as the temper won out. She paced a short circuit behind the couch, waving her hand at him. "It's like Keith Rimmer all over again. You just decided to handle it with no input from me."

Ty snorted. "He never bothered you again."

"You broke his nose!"

"He grabbed your ass. I was just supposed to let that go?"

Sebastian raised a hand. "Uh, did you two have an even busier few weeks than I realized?"

"High school," Paisley bit out. "He did it in high school."

"Wait, you two knew each other in high school?" Laurel asked.

"We dated for most of it." The array of Ohs that went around the room made Paisley wonder what Ty might have said about her without using her actual name. That was a question for another time. "In case it's escaped your notice, we aren't in high school anymore, Tyson. I'm not yours to protect."

He closed the distance between them so fast, she stumbled back a step. He didn't touch her, but she could feel the heat of temper rolling off him in waves. His voice was low, lethal. "If you think I'm capable of walking away again, you are sorely mistaken."

Her body leapt to attention at the promise and possession in his words. God, she wanted that. Wanted him. But she knew better than to trust it. He'd made it very clear after the wedding that he had nothing to offer.

Don't make promises you can't keep.

The words hovered on the tip of her tongue. But that would show her hand, and she didn't know if this urgency she felt from him would last once the danger was past. Needing to get back on some kind of even keel, she dug deep to find something—anything—that would diffuse a little of this desperate, vibrating tension between them. "You're a lot bossier than you were at eighteen."

A hint of humor flickered in his eyes. "Blame the Army."

Her lips twitched. She didn't want to leave him, didn't want to go home. A forced-proximity situation wasn't the most ideal way to explore things with him, but it was the opportunity she had. She wouldn't waste it. "Fine, since you *asked* so sweetly, I'll stay."

Ty's posture relaxed as he visibly dropped from DEFCON 1. "I'll work on the bossy thing."

She could imagine other scenarios where that wouldn't be such a bad thing. "Yeah, we'll talk about that later, too." Giving in to the need to touch him, she patted his chest. "Meanwhile, if you want me to spill my guts, you're going to have to feed me. I believe I was promised nachos."

"Yes, ma'am." He skimmed a thumb over her cheek, making her heart jump, even as she reflexively turned into the touch.

His eyes searched hers for another long moment before he turned away, wiping the emotion from his face. "Y'all eaten?"

Paisley didn't actually hear their responses. She was too busy trying to catch her breath. Duke trotted over, leaning against her legs and head-butting her hand to demand pets. She buried her trembling fingers in his fur.

As Ty moved to the kitchen, Ivy wandered over, murmuring *sotto voce*, "Lucy, you got some 'splaining to do."

"See," Sebastian insisted. "He *smiled*."

Laurel poked him in the ribs.

"Keep it up, Donnelly, and you forfeit your dinner rations," Ty called from the kitchen.

"Just callin' it like I see it."

Because she still felt a little shaky, Paisley circled around and dropped onto the sofa. Duke sprawled at her feet. "Okay, so, not that I don't appreciate the collective support, but I'm not exactly clear on why you're all here."

"Ty called, we came," Sebastian said simply. "It's what brothers do."

"And because, collectively, we can bring to bear considerably more brain power than has likely been devoted to your case by Metro PD," Harrison added. "I guarantee *they* haven't had a profiler look at your situation."

"Profiler?"

Ivy took a seat, leaning against her husband and looking faintly embarrassed as she raised her hand.

"I thought your degree was in psychology."

"Forensic psychology. I originally intended to go into the FBI before I decided I preferred dealing with murder on paper."

Paisley stared. "How did I not know this about you?"

"Never came up. Plenty from our pasts hasn't." She shot a pointed glance at Ty.

"Subtle," Paisley muttered. "And don't think I won't remember this next time I get a wild hair to write romantic suspense."

"Noted. But for now, what's going on?"

"I don't actually know where to start. It's hard to say what the beginning was."

"What's the first thing that gave you hinky vibes?" Laurel offered her own wry smile. "Recovering attorney."

"There were packages to my P.O. Box. The contents weren't overtly threatening, but they struck me as odd. Usually, when fans send me stuff—which isn't all that often—there's a letter that comes with it, gushing about my books and telling me about why they think I'll like whatever it is they sent. It's lovely, really. But this wasn't that. They were anonymous. No return address, no signature. No explanation at all. Just this printed card with 'Your biggest fan' on it. Maybe I've read *Misery* one too many times. I told myself I was being paranoid after I got mugged. Looking for conspiracies that weren't there."

"You got mugged?" Guard dog Ty was back, handing her a beer. "When?"

She sipped to wet the throat gone dry. "Back in July. Classic attacked in a parking garage situation by a guy in a ski mask. I wasn't hurt, really. Just scared. He got away with my purse. I reported it to the police, of course, but nothing ever came of it. There weren't any cameras and no leads to follow."

"When did the packages start?" Harrison asked.

"About four months ago."

"What made you decide to go to the police?" Laurel asked.

"I didn't go to them initially. I mean, what was I going to say? Someone is anonymously sending me Starbucks gift cards and my favorite tea, and I'm freaked out about it? It was mostly just a feeling of...something being off. Then one day I ran into a police contact of mine at the post office when I went to pick up my mail. There was another package. He saw my face and asked about it."

"Fisher," Ty concluded.

"Yes."

He finished passing out beverages to everyone else. "How exactly do you know him?"

Not Detective Fisher. Just a surname. Paisley wondered if he recognized that shade of green he was wearing. "Joel is one of the instructors from the citizen's police academy I took last year."

Ty frowned. "Why did you go to a citizen's police academy?"

"Book research. I thought it would help me make some connections with actual law enforcement who would let me pick their brains for plot purposes. Which it did. I got a friend in the crime lab out of it, too." She shrugged. "Anyway, I told him I had the heebee-jeebees, and he said he'd open a case, just to be safe. I really appreciated the fact that he didn't tell me I was crazy. When the package turned out to be a Funko Pop! Jessica Fletcher, I was back to thinking I was just paranoid."

"The chick from *Murder, She Wrote?*" Ivy asked.

"Yeah."

"You always loved that show," Ty murmured.

"Still do. I watch reruns when I can't sleep, which I've probably mentioned on social media at some point or other. It was, in a sense, thoughtful. But more came. One here. Two there. And then, a couple of weeks ago, I got the first mailed directly to my house."

"Somebody found out your home address," Sebastian observed.

"I don't use a pen name. A determined person with reasonable computer skills can find it. But nobody ever *has* before. It freaked me out, so Joel had Rico—he's my pal in the crime lab—go over it, but there was no trace evidence that could lead any-where. He said that since there weren't any overt threats and no actual laws had been broken, there was basically nothing he could do. I got home from *that* conversation to find another one sitting on my doorstep. No address at all. Just placed dead center of my welcome mat. That one was the collar I found on Duke. After that, I decided it would be prudent to get the hell out of town."

Ty crossed his arms and glowered. "You should have told me."

"Growling at me about it isn't going to change the fact that I didn't, so stop."

Ivy narrowed her eyes. "It's odd. As you say, nothing seems overtly threatening, but it sounds like each one has gotten a little more personal. Like the sender is saying 'Look, see, I know you.' And certainly, the switch from the P.O. Box to showing up at your house would have been wor-risome on its own. But it's a gigantic leap to go from packages, to breaking in, to finding you here. There's frustration in the action. You clearly weren't behaving in the way the sender wanted or anticipated. The question is, what do they want?"

"I think the more immediate question is whether she was followed directly or tracked."

Paisley felt the blood drain from her face again as Ty's words sank in. She hadn't had time to think that far. "I don't see how I could have been followed directly. It would have taken time to get into the house to retrieve the collar. And I spent nearly an hour driving around the city before I even left town, just in case someone was watching."

He made that growling noise again, and Paisley just pointed at him in warning. "I felt stupid when I did it."

"Clearly your instincts are better than your logical brain. Give me your phone. I'll check it for tracking software."

Harrison and Sebastian rose. "We'll sweep her car."

Paisley wondered how exactly this had become her life, where three highly trained former Rangers were suddenly in charge of her personal security.

Laurel shoved to her feet. "Well, clearly not charring dinner is going to be on us. Come on, ladies. We'll all think better with food."

Ivy stood, too. "Just keep the onions away from me. The smell has been turning me green."

Paisley looked up from digging in her purse for

the car keys. "Since when? You're the only person I know who loves French onion soup as much as I do." Her gaze zeroed in on the ginger ale in Ivy's hand instead of the beer everyone else was drinking and realization dawned. She hadn't imagined it possible to smile after the events of the night. "Seems I'm not the only one with some 'splaining to do."

"IT'S SUBTLE, but you can just see the scratches here."

Ty crouched down, examining the minute signs of lock picking Joel Fisher pointed at with a pencil. "That's the only signs we've got?"

The detective straightened, crossing his arms. "There's a partial footprint by the back fence, but with all the rain we had a couple days ago, any tread is entirely obscured. We can't even get a good estimate on size. Only prints on the door are Miss Parish's. Officers canvased the neighborhood, but nobody reported seeing anything."

"Maybe there will be something more inside. You haven't been in?"

Tall, with a rangy build and a craggy face that spoke of a lot of time outdoors, Fisher shook his head. Ty pegged him around mid-forties, though the job had added some years to that.

"Wanted to wait on Miss Parish and her key rather than doing any more damage or potentially obscuring evidence."

"Any *more* damage? Did they ransack my house?" Paisley's voice shot up half an octave.

"No, no!" Fisher soothed. "We didn't see any evidence of that through the windows. But we didn't see any need to bust in the door either."

"Oh. Well, can we go inside now and see whatever there is to see?"

He held out a hand toward the gate that led back around to the front of the bungalow. "After you."

Together they trooped around and up the steps to the front door. It was a hell of a different experience than the last time Ty had been here. That night, the only thing on his mind had been the miracle of running back into to Paisley after all these years and finding his way into her bed. He was in mission mode now.

Once she'd unlocked the door, he laid a hand on her shoulder. "Let us go in first and sweep the place. I don't expect anybody to be here, but just to be safe."

Fisher stepped into position, and Ty opened

the door. The alarm tone countdown sounded as he slipped inside.

"Alarm's still set."

Ignoring his order, Paisley ducked around him and made a beeline for the panel on the wall, punching in a code to disarm it.

"If they came in the back door, why didn't the alarm go off for the intruder?" Were they going to find the collar she'd received exactly where she left it? Had there been a duplicate just to freak her out?

Paisley bit her lip. "Um...there's no sensor on the back door."

"What do you mean there's no sensor?" Fisher demanded.

"Well, there was originally, but I kept forgetting about it and setting it off when I let Duke out in the morning, so I had it disabled."

Ty stared at her. "Are you kidding me?"

Her cheeks flushed. "You know I'm not a morning person."

He and Fisher exchanged a can-you-believe-this look, and Ty filed that under things to deal with later. With a shake of his head, he resumed the sweep.

No one was in the house. Nothing had been ransacked.

Fisher holstered his service weapon. "Is anything missing?"

"I don't know. I don't see anything right off-hand. The electronics are still here."

"Whoever broke in didn't come for electronics," Ty pointed out. "Where did you have the collar stored?"

She led them to a back bedroom and opened the closet. "Since I started getting creeped out, I put everything in this..." She trailed off, rising to her toes and running both hands along a shelf. "The box is gone. Everything I still had was in there."

"And yet nothing looks disturbed," Ty observed. "Almost like somebody knew exactly where it was."

Fisher rocked back on his heels. "Did you tell anyone where you were keeping the stuff?"

"No. Almost nobody knows about the problem at all."

Ty didn't like it. Last night they hadn't found a tracker on her phone or car or anywhere in her things. But if the perpetrator was close enough to lay hands on the dog, he could have removed it. It's what he would've done.

"Maybe there are cameras. Bugs. Something that would've told our perp where to look."

"Cameras!" Paisley crossed both arms tight over her middle, her cheeks going pale. She was just getting one hit after another.

Wishing he'd kept the idea to himself, Ty curved his hands around her shoulders, aware of Fisher's speculative gaze. "It's just another avenue to check. Why don't you go on and start packing?"

"Yeah, okay."

They waited until Paisley had made her way down the hall.

"She's going back to Eden's Ridge?"

He knew what Fisher was asking. Much as he wanted to stake his claim, he needed to be a cop here first. "She's got friends there. Let's search the place."

An hour and a half later, Fisher screwed the last air vent cover back in place. "Nothing. Hopefully that'll put Paisley more at ease."

"Maybe. But if someone broke in to take the evidence, it wouldn't be hard to pull any surveillance equipment as well." He'd have preferred to do an electronic sweep rather than a manual one, but he didn't have access to that kind of equipment now, and in all likelihood, their stalker wouldn't have access to the kind that would be easy to hide.

"Come on. Do you really think that's what happened?"

"You have a better theory?"

Fisher shot a glance toward the front of the house, where Paisley had disappeared, and dropped his voice. "I'm just saying, it's awfully convenient that I tell her I can't do anything with what I've got so far, and we suddenly have a big jump from mailing shit to dropping off a package in person, to alleged breaking and entering, to someone following her. Why the escalation?"

"You're suggesting she's making this up?" If that's where this guy's head was, no wonder there'd been no progress on her case.

"I don't want to think that. I really don't. I like her. She's a sweetheart. But I know she's frustrated as hell with the lack of progress, and I've gotta look at the facts in front of me: The alarm didn't go off. The scratches on the back door could just be from regular use. And Duke wasn't actually hurt, right? All we've got is her word that the collar came from here."

Bristling on Paisley's behalf, Ty drew on the control he'd learned as a soldier. "She's not lying to try to spark more action out of the police."

"Like I said, I don't want to think that. But Occam's Razor, man. What you're suggesting just seems like a lot of cloak and dagger shit that's more like something out of a book or movie when, up to now, the whole situation has looked like a simple case of an over-obsessed fan."

"The simplest explanation isn't always the right one. I was with her when she saw that collar. She was legit terrified someone had gotten to her dog."

"How do you know she's not a stellar actress?"

"Because I've known her for more than twenty years. She wasn't faking. I don't know what's going on or why, but I'm not discounting any possibility yet."

"Fair point. Please don't assume I'm not taking this seriously. I am. Have from the start. But you have to admit, there's not a lot to go on."

"No." And if this had been anyone else, he might have shared the same concerns. But this was Paisley. "What about the mugger?"

"Unrelated, as far as we could tell. It was months before she started getting packages. And why would some guy start with an attack on her person, then switch to something so low-key as random packages? Doesn't fit."

Ty nodded in acknowledgment. "I'd appreciate if you'd send me copies of your file. Maybe a fresh set of eyes will help."

"Of course. Whatever I can do to help. And I'll make sure to have patrols continue in the area. Though with the damned back door not hooked in, I don't know how helpful that will be."

More than done with Fisher, Ty straightened. "I'll take care of it." He'd be plugging a number of other holes in her security before they left town.

"Good. I'll feel better knowing she's got a properly secured house. I'll send that file as soon as I get back to the station."

"Appreciate it."

After Fisher left, Ty went in search of Paisley. She sat in her office, hugging a pillow and staring at nothing.

"Paisley?"

"What if someone's been watching me all this time, Ty? When I thought I was alone? Do you have any idea how disturbing that is?"

"We didn't find any evidence of that or anything else." He felt bad enough for mentioning the possibility to her. He sure as hell wasn't offering up his theory that there might have been something that had been removed.

"I'm not sure it makes a difference either way, at this point. My home, my sanctuary, has been violated. I don't know how to get over that."

"With time and answers. Meanwhile, you'll be

safe with me." He'd make sure of it. "How's the packing coming?"

She lifted haunted eyes to his. "I'm basically done. It's all in the foyer."

Ty glanced behind him, expecting to see a small mountain. But there were only a few boxes and more stuff for Duke. Was she trying to pack light, or did she expect this to be a short cohabitation? With everything that had happened in the past twenty-four hours, she probably didn't know what to think. Hell, neither did he. He just knew he'd do whatever he had to in order to keep her safe.

"How about packing up any food that's going to spoil? We'll take that back with us, too. I'll load this in the truck."

She rose from her chair with none of her usual buoyancy. Her light had gone out, and he *hated* seeing it. Nothing should ever dim that light. Short of hunting down the one harassing her, what the hell could he do to give back that spark? It wasn't like he could just flip a switch. Hell, he knew that better than anybody.

She'd need time and support. He was determined to give her both.

8

"You've been quiet the whole drive. I can hear your wheels spinning over there."

Paisley didn't look at Ty as they made the final turn onto his road. He'd stayed silent since they left Nashville, leaving her to her thoughts. They hadn't been good ones. Exhausted and emotional, she was still processing the fact that her sense of safety had been utterly shattered. Thanks to Ty, her house had been secured, but even when all this was over—whenever that might be—she didn't know if she'd ever be able to really *live* in her little bungalow again. How did she overcome that sense it would never actually be safe?

"I don't know what to say. I don't even know what exactly it is you're going to *do*, when there's no real evidence and apparently Joel thinks I'm making all this latest stuff up." And damn, that stung. She'd thought they were some manner of friends.

"Heard him, huh?"

"And I heard you defending me. I appreciate that."

"I've got your back in this, Pais. I've got resources he doesn't have and certainly more motivation to get to the bottom of it."

"I'm sure you'll be glad to have your space back when this is all over."

"Hey." He reached across the console of the truck, curling his hand around hers. "That's *not* the motivation."

When he didn't continue, she was too afraid to ask what his reason actually was. If it was anything related to pity, she didn't think she could take it. She didn't want to think about him having her back. Didn't want to start depending on him. She well knew where that led. This was a temporary aberration. She was a job for him. Sort of.

As they pulled into the driveway, Duke scrambled up, shoving his nose between the seats. He'd had a full day hanging out on Sebastian and Laurel's farm and had been napping in the backseat. Curling her arm around him, she relaxed a bit as he wriggled and head-butted his adoration. Her boy could always be counted on to lift her mood. He was an endless supply of joy.

"Let's get unloaded." Ty slid out of the truck and began hefting boxes from the bed.

Paisley sprang Duke from the back, snapping on a leash so he didn't go racing off into the woods. In all likelihood, no one was out there, but she wasn't about to take any chances. Ty was already on the third load by the time she ordered Duke to his bed by the wood stove. He circled four times and plopped down with a contented sigh. She only wished she could be as comfortable here as her dog. But she didn't know where she fit or even if she fit. Right now, her own skin felt wrong, as if she'd suddenly been thrust into someone else's body, someone else's life.

Once they'd brought everything in, she shouldered the duffel bag she'd loaded with clothes and started up the stairs.

"You don't have to do that now. It's been a long day."

"For the sake of our shins and the navigability of the floor, I really do." Besides, she needed something to distract herself from how weird she felt about all of this.

"There's space in the dresser and part of the closet."

Paisley paused, glancing down at him. Had he cleared space for her when she wasn't looking or did he just have that little stuff? "Thanks."

Dropping the bag on the bed, she located the space meant for her and began putting away clothes, her mind spinning anew on the questions she'd been mulling the whole way back to Eden's Ridge.

Visiting for the weekend was one thing, but actually living with him for an undetermined amount of time was something else entirely. True cohabitation meant no keeping things surface, no hiding from each other, especially in a place this small. What happened if he got sick of her? She was already having issues with blurred lines because of their history. For her own sanity, maybe they needed to have a conversation to clarify the boundaries. She needed a reminder of what this really was between them. A temporary thing. Real life, not one of those bodyguard romances she loved. She could manage her expectations. She'd been managing expectations of her relationships for years.

With that in mind, she headed back downstairs, pulling on her mental armor for what she considered a necessary conversation.

Ty was digging through a box himself. He straightened, a couple of pillows in hand. Bright, cheerful pillows that normally lived on her living room sofa. He tossed them onto his, and she noticed the fuzzy throw from her office. Looking around, she spotted the Queen of Awesomeness mug full of her favorite pens sitting on the side table where she'd been working yesterday, and the insulated coffee mug Emerson had bought her because she kept forgetting she'd made tea and letting it get cold.

She hadn't packed any of it. "What is all this?"

Scrubbing a hand over the back of his neck, he shrugged. "This whole situation is hard on you. I want you to feel comfortable here. My place isn't exactly...homey, so I packed some of the stuff it looked like you use all the time."

Paisley stared at him, at the whole other box of stuff still waiting beside him. She and her problem had invaded his life, inconvenienced him in countless ways, and in response, he'd tried to bring some of her home to his.

Something inside her broke. The opaque glass wall of denial surrounding the truth she'd been hiding from. There would be no managing of expectations. Because she was in love with him. Again. Or maybe still. Ty Brooks was her person. The one she'd been looking for and writing about for eighteen years, just waiting for him to come back to her. And now here he was, doing this devastatingly sweet thing, and she didn't even know where he stood on the topic of them.

She burst into tears.

The blur of Ty moved into her field of vision, reaching for her. He pulled her in tight, wrapping those big, strong, capable arms around her, and all she wanted to do was lean on him. "I'm sorry I didn't ask first. I thought you'd be okay with it. We can pack it back up. You don't have to look at it."

Under any other circumstances, the edge of panic in his voice might have made her smile. Instead, she sobbed harder, pressing her face against his chest. "No, I'm not mad. It's sweet and thoughtful."

His broad palm cradled her head. "Then what are you upset about, baby?"

"How the hell am I supposed to keep my head in this short-term, casual zone when you're acting like this?" she demanded, hiccupping through another sob. A part of her wanted to pound against his chest, but that would require letting go of the death grip she had on his shirt.

"Like what?"

"Like the sweet, thoughtful, caring boyfriend you used to be." Realizing the heaving breaths weren't helping her be understood, she fought for some measure of calm. "I don't know how to not feel around you. I asked for casual. I agreed to casual. I'm trying so hard not to change the rules, but you're making it so fucking *hard*."

The tension in his frame relaxed as he leaned back and tipped her face up. His hand was gentle as he thumbed away her tears. "We were fooling ourselves that this was ever going to be casual. It's not who we were, not who we *are*. There's something here, Paisley. There always was."

That shocked her enough to stem the tears. Her heart kicked hard and fast against her ribs. "What are you saying?" She needed him to spell it out for her so she didn't take a leap without a net.

He cupped her cheek in his broad, callused palm. "I'm saying let's change the rules."

IT SCARED the shit out of Ty to say it. No part of him felt like he deserved the gift of another chance with her. He wasn't at all sure he could do more, but he knew without a doubt he couldn't do less. If this time with her had showed him anything, it was that he couldn't do casual with her. He couldn't be with this woman and not remember what used to be.

She made him want to protect her, to be the one she could turn to. He wanted to be the one to take that fear away for her. With every part of his battered, battle-scarred soul, he wanted to earn her love again because it was the color, the joy he'd been missing for half his life, and he was more afraid of having to learn how to do without it again than he was of not trying at all.

Throughout the past few weeks, she'd slipped in and out of this unfamiliar, guarded demeanor, as if she'd kept reminding herself of the rules she'd mentioned. And maybe she had. But all traces of that emotional armor were gone now.

"I'm going to need you to spell this out for me because I want to make sure I don't misunderstand."

The tearful, tremulous hope dawning on her face twisted Ty into knots. He'd hurt her so badly before. He was determined that he wouldn't—couldn't do it again. That would take more honesty, more bravery, than he'd given her in years.

Because he needed to keep touching her, he cupped her jaw, his fingers pressing against the fluttering pulse in her throat. "I had to walk away from you after high school because I knew we wouldn't survive my constant deployment, and I wouldn't be able to do the job the way I needed to because a part of me would have been back home with you. I thought it was better if you had the chance to move on and build the life you wanted. One with somebody else, who wouldn't always be half a world away. Garrett never let me forget how much of a fool he thought that made me." Ty swallowed, thinking perhaps he was finally doing something his brother of the heart would approve of.

"Maybe I was wrong. Maybe I wasn't. But I never expected to have you back in my life. Running into you again has been like a damned miracle. I stopped even hoping for those a long damned time ago. But the fact is, we have a second chance—if you're willing—and I don't want to waste it. I can't make any promises of smooth sailing. My service changed me, and I've got shit that will never fully heal. But you make me remember who I used to be, who *we* used to be, and I want that. I want you. I always wanted you." The pulse beneath his fingers leapt.

"Ty." Paisley's voice was choked, and he realized she was crying again.

Before he could give in to the fresh spate of panic that he'd said the wrong thing again, she rose to her toes and kissed him. "Yes." And again. "Yes." Her hands wove into his hair, and she pressed her brow to his. "Yes."

Relieved and knowing he was luckier than he had any right to be, Ty held her tighter. "I've missed you so damned much." Brushing his mouth to hers, he began to back her toward the sofa. "Let me show you."

He felt the flutter of a smile against his lips as she murmured, "Dog."

Right. He wasn't used to working around one.

A quick glance told him Duke was already snoozing on his bed, but Ty wasn't keen on canine interruptus, so he switched directions, moving them toward the stairs, wishing for a more normal set he could carry her up to give her a little romance. She deserved romance. She deserved everything.

They climbed to the loft and reached for each other. Her mouth met his again and again as they slowly undressed, exploring each inch of newly revealed skin. He didn't want frantic or hurried. He wanted to make love to her as she deserved, slow and thorough, to give them both the gift of time.

Paisley lay back on the bed, pulling him down

and over her with a sigh. Her hair pooled against the pillow, a silky mass of waves begging for his fingers. He lost himself in the scent and taste of her, gorging himself on the feel of her bare skin. His own system sparked and trembled as she touched and took, reclaiming him in a way he'd never wanted with anyone else. With her hands and mouth, she soothed the scars, no question, no hesitation in her movements. Every touch was an acceptance of who he was now, an acknowledgment of all he'd endured in their years apart.

His eyes met hers as he slipped inside her and found welcome. When they would have blurred and closed with passion, he held on, curling his hands with hers where they pressed against the mattress. "Stay with me."

"Yes." She rose to meet him. Every sinuous move of her body echoed the word, a hundred affirmations that buoyed the heart he'd thought too damaged to ever beat for someone else again. It pounded for her as he stroked deeper, driving them up and up, on a long, languid climb he wanted to make forever.

Then she sighed his name, her body shuddering over the edge and pulling him into the slippery fall of an endless, glorious release. He poured himself into her, emptying all the heartbreak and loss and lonely years, until his tarnished soul felt cleansed, and they were both laid bare.

Afterward, they lay tangled and spent, hearts thudding, skin cooling. Her fingers stroked down his nape in a hypnotic rhythm. He pressed a kiss to her shoulder, absorbing her hum of pleasure, and for the first time in more years than he could count, he felt at peace.

9

"There's so little here." Discouraged, Paisley dropped her copy of the thin file Joel had sent and rubbed at the headache beginning to bloom.

"There's more here than you think. And your own pictures and notes will help make up for the theft of the original packages." Ty's hand settled on her nape and began to knead.

Paisley couldn't stop the quiet sound of relief or the way her body automatically leaned into his touch. He pressed a kiss to her temple, and she caught the shared glances between the rest of his friends scattered around Harrison and Ivy's living room for this sitrep meeting.

Last night had changed everything. They'd

both stopped fighting the pull between them. She'd worried he'd be uncomfortable about it around the others, but it was as if a switch had been flipped, setting him to Boyfriend Mode. It was weird and wonderful and clearly out of character for him based on how everyone kept staring. This was her Ty, and they were just going to have to get used to it.

For once, Sebastian kept his mouth shut, but he did offer her a thumbs up when Ty appeared not to be looking. Even as Paisley's lips twitched, Ty flipped him off and continued to massage her neck and shoulders.

"Children," Ivy warned.

"Awww, look at you, practicing your mom voice," Paisley teased.

"These three clowns give me plenty of opportunity." She spread a look between the three men. "Anyway, Ty's right. There's enough here to help us build a timeline. Once we have that, we'll look at what else was going on in your life at the time to see if we can map what might have sparked the changes."

Wielding a dry erase marker on the massive whiteboard Paisley knew she used for book plotting, Ivy made notes. Together, they slowly, painstakingly reconstructed the entire thing, with notes about each contact. By the time they'd finished, it was easy to see the progression delineated.

Ty added the last one to a digital map on his computer. "There were different postmarks on all of them. Each one is within about an hour's drive of Nashville proper, so it seems likely that whoever's doing the sending lives or works within or close to that radius."

Ivy studied the whiteboard. "Everything kept a degree of separation until a little over two weeks ago. That's when things got more direct. What was going on two-and-half weeks ago?"

Paisley considered. "Nothing unusual, other than your wedding. But I don't see what that would have to do with anything."

"Not just the wedding," Ty said. "Me. You left the reception with me."

And she'd taken him home with her.

"The first direct-to-your-house package showed up the following Monday," Ivy continued. "The first one with no note, like maybe it wasn't thought out but reactionary."

"Like maybe someone was jealous?" Harrison put in.

"It seems like a reasonable argument that the person behind this is, if not definitely male, probably interested," Laurel added. "Ty would represent a threat in that case."

Paisley frowned. "I have a hard time imagining a guy doing the rest of this."

"The other day, when you saw the collar, you said 'he'. 'He followed me.' Why?"

"It wasn't a conscious choice of pronoun. I guess I don't tend to see women as a threat. And we thought, before that, that it was likely a fan. Or...I did. Detective Fisher ran with that theory."

"You have male fans," Ty pointed out.

She thought of those well-worn copies of her books back at his place. "Yeah, I suppose I do. Though it's definitely not the majority."

"You should check out our guest list and the registry book from the wedding," Harrison suggested. "Not everybody signed it, and we can't account for all of the plus ones, but maybe you'll recognize somebody's name."

"We should also cross reference those names with the people on her mailing list and those who follow her on social media," Ivy said.

They collectively split up the task and began combing through. Paisley started with the guest book Harrison brought. After all her years in Nashville, she recognized a lot of names, but no one she had a particular connection to. Laurel picked out four women who definitely subscribed to Paisley's newsletter, and Ivy found a couple more who might follow her on social media. None seemed like viable candidates for her stalker.

"What about pictures?" Sebastian asked. "That photographer was all over the place, snapping pictures of everybody. Maybe Paisley will see someone she recognizes."

"We just got the gallery of proofs back." Harrison retrieved a sleek little MacBook and logged into the photographer's website.

Paisley scrolled through the online gallery, feeling a bittersweet mix of joy and yearning as she checked out the play-by-play of Ivy and Harrison's big day. They'd looked so blissfully happy and perfect together. They *were* blissfully happy and perfect together, building the life and the future they wanted.

She was still too scared to let herself dream of that. It had been so many years since she'd allowed herself to want that kind of a future. After all the disappointments and failures, it had seemed safer to tuck those desires away and enjoy what was right in front of her. And she did enjoy the heady bliss of a new relationship. But it had been a long time since she could fully throw herself headlong into the pursuit of romance. Maybe because she was more battered and bruised than she wanted to admit from all the deliberate attempts to fall in love. Love wasn't a thing to be forced, like a flower bulb in winter.

As she saw her own face on the screen, turned up to Ty's while they danced, she couldn't help thinking that love bloomed where it was planted... and hers had been planted for this man when they were only sixteen.

"What about that guy?" Ty asked.

Pulled out of her thoughts, Paisley looked to where he pointed. In the periphery of the shot, the man who'd hit on her at the reception glared in their direction. "He looks mad enough to spit nails. But I'd never met him before that night. I never even got his name. He was too busy offering up bad pickup lines, and then you gallantly rode to my rescue."

"He was hitting on virtually anything with a skirt and getting shot down at every turn. I watched him working the room before he got to you."

"Why did you intervene? You didn't know it was me."

"He had you cornered, and I know a predator when I see one."

Ivy leaned over the back of the couch to look at

the screen. "Oh, that's Glen Bartlett. He's a distant cousin who is a pox on womankind. We didn't actually invite him, but my great aunt brought him anyway as her plus one and chauffeur. I think she was under the delusion that he might meet a nice girl. She keeps thinking it will settle him down, but he's not the type to be capable of love, let alone change for it."

"We'll add him to the list of people to follow up on."

Paisley scrolled through the rest of the pictures. As before, she knew quite a few people, but none who seemed a decent candidate for a stalker.

Ty set the laptop on the coffee table. "So, for this theory to hold, either someone at the wedding we aren't aware of saw us together or someone saw us together at some point after."

"You're suggesting I was being followed even then?" The idea had gooseflesh rising on Paisley's arms.

"Maybe. Or there might be some other trigger for the shift that we haven't thought of yet."

"Thinking back over the past few months, have there been points where you were uneasy? Where you felt like there were eyes on you or that something wasn't right?" Ivy asked.

"Plenty. But I just thought I was being paranoid after being mugged."

"It could be that. Or it could be that you're picking up on more than you're aware of. The fact is, whoever is behind this is watching you in some form or fashion. On social media. Through your books. They've done enough digging to uncover your home address. That might have been by looking through records, or it might have been by tailing you. You've had public appearances, book signings. It wouldn't be that hard to stick around and follow you home."

"If you're trying to scare me further, you're doing a damned good job of it."

Ty squeezed her shoulders. "Nobody's getting to you here. And I'm not so sure it's someone random. Did Fisher ever look at your exes?"

Paisley wasn't keen on talking about her past dating history with Ty. "No reason to, we thought. I parted on good terms with most of them."

He grunted a noncommittal noise. "I think it's worth looking at. These are guys who do know you on a certain level. Or thought they did. That's something of a gift of yours."

"What is?"

"Making people think they're closer to you than they are. You're so warm and friendly, and you really listen to people. That kind of attention is...intoxicating. You remember what it was like in high school, how many people thought you were their bestie."

"So now it's a problem that I'm nice to people?"

"No. Not at all. I'm just saying that someone could have misinterpreted that behavior, maybe thought your relationship was more serious than it was. Can you make a list tracing back your relationship history?"

"Why?"

"These gifts show an inherent base-level knowledge of you. Stands to reason somebody who's jealous of you being involved with someone might have enjoyed the privilege himself and want that back."

"Then why not just ask me?"

"Maybe you said no. Or maybe it was a long game that I screwed up. Either way, I think the list could be useful."

Paisley could see his point, but she didn't like it. "How far back am I supposed to go?"

"Is it that long a list in total?"

Stiffening, she pulled away, hating the flush she felt in her cheeks. She'd been a serial monogamist for years. She wasn't ashamed of that, damn it. "I like dating, and I've done a lot of it."

"I think we could all do with some snacks," Laurel announced. "Boys, why don't you come help in the kitchen?"

It was a thin excuse to give them some privacy, but as everyone else filed out, Paisley blessed Laurel for the gesture. She rose herself and paced over to stare sightlessly at the whiteboard. She could feel Ty's gaze on her.

"I wasn't a monk the last eighteen years. I don't expect you were either."

"I didn't sleep with all of them."

"Okay. Even if you had, it would've been your right. It's your life, your body. We weren't together then. I'm not judging you here. I'm just trying to work one angle. If it helps, for now, limit it to the ones you broke up with."

That list was shorter and easier to produce. She wrote it out, making notations where she could about how long she'd spent in each relationship, and handed it over. "It's probably not all of them. I don't remember every guy I ever went on a date with and didn't go for a second. If we need more, I can call Emerson and brainstorm with her."

"Emerson?"

"We've been best friends since college. She's been around for most of my dating career."

"I can probably help fill in some gaps too," Ivy added, coming back in carrying drinks. "At least for the last couple of years, which would probably be the most relevant."

The others filed behind her with bowls and platters of food. There was a veggie tray, chips and dip, popcorn, and someone had put together a charcuterie board.

"This is fine." Ty sat again, studying the list.

Paisley began loading a plate. Maybe if she stuffed her face, she wouldn't be so prone to letting her mouth run away with her. Objectively, she understood why he was pursuing this line of investigation. But she didn't have to like it.

"You were the one who called it quits on both your marriages?"

"Yeah."

"What happened there? Infidelity? Money problems?"

"No. Nothing like that."

"Then what?"

"I don't see why it matters."

"Because I'm trying to find a motive."

"Neither of my ex-husbands is behind this."

"You don't know that. We'll need to look at them, and in doing so I need to know why you broke things off."

Paisley set her plate down and crossed the room to the picture window, staring out at the mountain. She *hated* having her relationships put under a microscope.

"Were they abusive?" Ty's voice was quiet and right behind her.

"No, they're both good guys."

"Then what?"

"They weren't you," she whispered.

"What?"

Exasperated, embarrassed, and knowing he'd find out eventually, she whirled on him. "They weren't you, okay? Every single relationship I've had for the last eighteen years has all ended for the same damned reason. Because I kept trying to find another you and failing. You ruined me for all men when we were eighteen. Congratulations."

Ty blinked at her for a moment before his lips began to twitch.

"Tyson Gregory Brooks, don't you dare *smile*. This is not meant as a stroke for your ego."

"She middle-named him," Sebastian whispered.

"Shh!" Laurel hissed.

The twitch turned into a full-on grin.

"If you say it's not your ego that wants stroking right now, I swear to God, I'm going to hit you."

They both ignored the chorus of choked laughter.

"Hey, you're the one whose brain went there."

"I write romance for a living. Of *course,* my brain went there. But this is not a joke."

He sobered, but there was a softness in his eyes in place of the humor as he reeled her in. "Does it help to know I hate them all on principle for getting time with you that I didn't?"

"Maybe. A little."

"How about the fact that there's never been anyone serious for me but you?"

It was Paisley's turn to blink. "Never?"

"I was married to the job, and I didn't have the strength of heart to put myself out there to even try. So, I'd say we mutually ruined each other."

Someone behind them sniffed. "That is just the sweetest..."

"Are you crying?" Harrison asked his wife.

"Pregnancy hormones. I'm allowed. Shut up and pass the popcorn."

THEY SPLIT THE WORK. As the resident cop with any actual authority to request alibis, Ty hit up the phone for the guys they had contact information on, while everyone else worked on tracking down the others on Paisley's list. For privacy's sake, he holed up in Harrison's office. Deciding to get the ex-husbands over with first, he reviewed the brief dossiers Paisley had written.

Wasband Number 1: Brian Chesney

Ty actually smiled at her alternative name for ex-husband.

Chesney was the college boyfriend she'd married right after graduation. According to Paisley's notes, they'd lasted three years, divorcing at twenty-five. He now lived in Memphis with his second wife and their two kids. Given the postmarks of all the letters and packages, it was unlikely he was connected, but Ty wanted to do due diligence and call.

A woman answered the phone. "Hello?"

"I'm looking for Brian Chesney." In the background, Ty could hear the sounds of kids laughing.

"Just a minute."

A few moments later, a guy picked up. "Hello?"

"Brian Chesney?"

"Yeah." The voice was friendly, open.

"This is Deputy Ty Brooks with the Stone County Sheriff's Department. I have a few questions for you."

Chesney's tone hardened. "What's this about?"

"Your ex-wife, Paisley Parish."

"Hang on a second." Brian excused himself from whatever was going on and went somewhere quieter. "What's happened to Paisley? Is she all right?" Ty didn't miss the edge of protectiveness in the demand.

"She's okay. Having some trouble. Can you tell me your whereabouts on the weekend of January sixteenth?"

"Of course. My father-in-law just had a heart attack three weeks ago. Double bypass surgery. On that Saturday we were all in the waiting room at Baptist Memorial Hospital in Memphis. I've got half a dozen people who can verify. What is it you're checking me out for?"

"She's being stalked."

"Shit. I knew this would happen someday."

That piqued Ty's curiosity. "What makes you say that?"

"She's too nice. I don't know if you've spent much time with her with the investigation, but under normal circumstances, she's got this warm, magnetic personality. Spend five minutes with her on a good day and you feel like... I don't know. Like that song 'Walking on Sunshine'."

Ty huffed a laugh. "Yeah, she's always been like that."

There was a pause. "What did you say your name was?"

"Ty Brooks."

"*That* Ty Brooks?"

He went brows up. "I hesitate to say yes to that tone, but probably."

"Hm." There was a wealth of judgement in that single syllable. Ty wondered what she'd said about him. "She brought this problem to you?"

"More like it came to us. I'm investigating."

Chesney seemed to consider that. "Look, we've been divorced a long time. We're still friends. She sends my kids birthday presents every year. I want nothing but the best for her. If that's you, great. But for God's sake, don't fuck it up this time."

A blessing and a warning in the same breath. Not entirely sure what to do with that, Ty lost a little of his professionalism. "I'm tryin' not to. Thanks for your cooperation."

"If there's anything else I can do to help, please let me know."

Ty hung up and stared at his phone for a long minute. He hadn't anticipated the guy would recognize his name, know who he was. That was...weird. But maybe not. It was normal enough to talk about high school in college. She'd been a lot closer to the heartbreak when she'd met Brian. Still, it had Ty feeling a little bit paranoid as he checked the notes for Wasband Number 2.

Clint Mercer lived in Franklin, Tennessee. Unlike Number 1, he was close enough to have dropped the letters and packages around the city. They'd married when she was not quite thirty and lasted only a year. It seemed unlikely the guy would've popped back up after five years, but stranger things had happened.

No one answered Ty's call, so he left a voicemail and continued working his way down the list. He'd cleared three more names by the time Mercer called him back.

"I think you've got the wrong number, man. I haven't been anywhere near Stone County…actually I'm not sure I've ever been to Stone County."

"Did you used to be married to Paisley Parish?"

The affable attitude disappeared. "Yeah. Is she all right?"

Interesting that the first question from both of them was whether she was okay. "She's fine. I need to check your whereabouts in conjunction with an investigation." He gave the dates.

"I wasn't even in the country. I was on assignment in Belarus. My boss can confirm, and I've got flight records."

"What is it you do?

"I'm a photojournalist. You happened to catch me on break between stories. I'm flying back out tomorrow. What's going on with Paisley? Is she in some kind of trouble?"

"You could say that. How would you characterize your relationship with your ex-wife?"

"Brief and intense. We met when she was doing research on a book. I told her there was no better way to learn than on the job. I took her with me to Greece. We eloped before we came back to the States."

Of course, they had. Elopement seemed entirely in character for Paisley. She'd love the impulsivity and romance of it.

"She traveled with me on job for a while, but it wasn't conducive to her work, and she didn't handle the separation well when I was on long assignments."

"When you say didn't handle the separation well..."

Mercer blew out a breath. "She accused me of putting the job before her. Which was accurate. She wasn't okay with that, so we parted amicably after about a year."

That confirmed what Ty had long suspected and made him feel a little better about breaking things off with her before going into the Army. Deployment would've broken them.

"Do you keep in touch?" This wasn't their guy, but Ty found he wanted to know.

"Sure. I see her when I make it home when we're both free, and we keep up on social media."

Ty found himself wondering if those catch ups had been the naked kind. Had this guy inspired the casual stance she'd taken toward dating the last few years? Shaking his head, he told himself it didn't matter. She was with him now.

"Thanks for your, help. If I need anything else, I'll let you know."

"Before you go—are you the Ty she knew in high school?"

Really? Again? "Yeah."

"Yours is the name she calls for in her sleep. If you're finally crossing paths again, it seems like a thing you ought to know."

Ty sat and thought about that for a long time after hanging up. What was she dreaming about years after they'd split that she was calling out for him? Did she have nightmares? He didn't know why it bothered him, except that, on some level, she'd needed him, and he hadn't been there for her. He'd put his duty to his country, to his men, to Garrett first. He couldn't regret that. He'd saved lives, averted disaster more times than he could count. The work he'd done had mattered.

But that work was finished now. It was someone else's duty. And for the first time in forever, there was absolutely nothing he had to put before Paisley. He was here for her now, and he'd do whatever it took to make up for those years apart.

10

"I appreciate you letting me set up here today. Ty's probably being overcautious, but I'm still nervy about being by myself."

Ivy shut the door behind Paisley and bent to scrub Duke's ears. "It's no problem. Where better to hang out and write than a house with two other writers? Besides, now I can ask all my nosy questions."

"I knew that interrogation was coming." A part of her was glad of it. She had some of her own questions, and she didn't think she could ask Ty. "At least ply me with coffee first."

Ivy led the way toward the kitchen. "I will enjoy the second-hand coffee fumes."

"I thought pregnant women could have one cup a day?"

"Doc says yes. Baby says, Ha ha ha ha! No! I'm considering an espresso-scented candle."

"That might just make me sadder. Where's Harrison?"

"Already in the writing cave." Ivy pulled out a couple of mugs and gestured to the coffee pot before turning on the kettle for herself. "He still keeps early hours after all that time in the Army. He's usually had a run, breakfast, and his first hit of caffeine by the time I surface."

Grateful she didn't even have to wait for it to brew, Paisley poured herself a cup. "Ty was a morning person even before the Army. I'm reasonably sure that means he's from another planet. But he uses those hours to my benefit, so I can't really argue."

"Oh *really*?"

Paisley laughed. "I didn't mean that. Although yeah." She definitely couldn't argue with a sexy start to her morning, even if it meant she'd be jonesing for a nap by two. "He took me to school back in the day, and he'd always bring me coffee in a travel mug. And on Mondays, he'd stop and pick up donut holes so the morning would suck less."

"That's really sweet. I have to admit, I'm having

a hard time picturing high school Ty. The version I've known has always seemed...stony and taciturn."

"He was less serious, but still kind of quiet until you pulled him out of his shell, which I was really good at." Paisley sipped, smiling as much at the memory as the hit of delicious caffeine. "He had a chivalrous bent, even then. It's how we met, actually. I was the new girl in school that year. My parents were big into throwing me into the deep end to make friends, so I was at the Homecoming Dance alone, feeling awkward as hell. This asshole started hassling me, and Ty shows up with punch, pretending to be my boyfriend. So, I did what any red-blooded girl would do in that situation."

"Played along."

"I kissed him. At which point we both forgot about the asshole. It was a damned miracle Ty didn't spill the punch all over us both because I shocked the hell out of him."

"Wow. What happened to the asshole?"

"I don't know. I couldn't see anybody else after that because I'd just been struck by lightning. Ty's hair was practically smoking, so I knew I wasn't alone in that. I told him he was my hero and that was more or less it. We were just together after that. Back then I thought we always would be. He was my first love, and I couldn't ever imagine being with anyone else. I'd picked right, straight out of the gate."

Ivy joined her at the counter with a cup of tea. "I'm starting to understand how you became a romance writer."

"It was really great fodder for it, that's for sure." But it hadn't stayed that way. "After we graduated, I thought we had the whole summer ahead of us before we headed off to college. Garrett and Bethany got engaged, which was a shock to no one. They'd been together since the fourth grade. So, one night, Ty picks me up and takes me down to our spot by the river. There was this romantic picnic and Ty starts talking about the future and how much he loves me." Even remembering, Paisley's heart began to thrum with anticipation. "Any second, I was expecting him to get down on one knee and propose. And instead, he tells me he and Garrett have enlisted and that they're aiming for Special Forces. I thought I'd misheard him. We were leaving for college in two months. What the hell was he talking about? He went off on this whole tangent about duty. I didn't understand it. In my world there was absolutely nothing more important than love. It turned out this had been in discussion for months, and he hadn't said a word to me."

"Ouch! Was all the romance supposed to soften the blow?"

"He wanted to make it clear that making the decision to end things wasn't because he didn't care about me, which wasn't at all what it felt like at the time. And he wanted to talk me into staying together until it was time for him to go, making the most of the time we had left."

"Was that the end right there, or did you get your summer?"

"I held on. Did everything in my power to change his mind. In the end, nothing stopped him from getting on that bus."

"That must have been awful having him choose the Army over you."

"It was devastating. But it wasn't the Army he chose over me. It was Garrett. He's the only one Ty loved more than me. And I get it. They were brothers from diapers. Nothing was more important to him than having Garrett's back. Which isn't to say he didn't feel he had a duty to country, but I don't think it would have been strong enough to make him enlist on his own."

"Did you resent Garrett for that?"

"No. He didn't make Ty choose."

"He could have chosen to try to make it work."

"We wouldn't have made it. Ty understood that before I did. He made the right call for us under the circumstances. I would have made a lousy military wife. Which is a lot easier to say with the wisdom of years. But it didn't make it suck any less or any easier to let him go. I grieved for a really, really long time."

"And so, he became your hero archetype."

Paisley lifted her mug in a toast. "Got it in one."

"This explains so much about your work."

"I love me some second chance romance."

"Seems like you've got one. How did that happen anyway?"

"In a moment of glorious symmetry that I couldn't have plotted better myself, there was your asshole cousin at your reception, and Ty swept in with the exact same ploy, pretending to be my date."

Chin in hands, green eyes sparkling, Ivy grinned. "Did you kiss him again?"

"I did."

"And that, it seems, is the end of that. Again."

"Maybe."

"You two give off fireworks when you're in a room together. Why the lack of confidence?"

"We started out doing this whole casual thing."

Ivy snorted. "There is nothing casual about the way that man looks at you."

"I know. But this stalker situation pushed him when I don't know if he was ready to be pushed. I'm deathly afraid that this is Speed Syndrome."

"It's what now?"

"Like you're afraid, when the bus stops, everything will go kablooey?" Harrison supplied as he stepped into the kitchen and made straight for the coffee pot.

"Yes, exactly. And please, let's educate your wife about one of Keanu Reeves' best roles."

"It's not her fault. She was a toddler when that came out."

Paisley winced. "I keep forgetting you're so much younger than me."

"I think I understand the concept well enough. You think when the threat to you is gone, he'll balk."

"It's what I'm afraid of. This whole situation, combined with our history, has escalated things between us. And I'm not convinced that's a good thing."

Harrison and Ivy exchanged one of those married-people looks that told Paisley this was a topic they'd discussed.

"I have a different theory," Ivy offered.

"By all means, enlighten me."

"Do you know that before the last few days, I've never seen Ty smile?"

She'd heard the jokes but hadn't thought much about it. "That wasn't just Sebastian giving him shit?"

"No. I didn't meet him until he was already out of the service, after Garrett's death. He took it incredibly hard, as you'd expect."

"They were brothers, in every way that mattered," Paisley murmured. "I've still got friends back home, so I knew Garrett had died, but haven't asked Ty about it. I'm kind of afraid to. How bad was it?"

Harrison kicked back against the counter with a fresh cup of coffee. "Depression. PTSD. Suicide watch. He gave me a helluva shiner when I stopped him from eating a bullet."

She covered her mouth, already feeling tears begin to fall at the thought of it. So much pain and grief. No matter the circumstances, he'd blame himself because protecting Garrett was the whole reason he'd gone in. This was what he'd meant by wounds that would never heal.

"He shut himself off from everything and almost everyone. Getting him into law enforcement helped. It gave him a new purpose, and that brought him back from the brink. But he hasn't really been living. Everything but the job has been temporary. You've seen his place. He could move out tomorrow and you'd never even know he was there."

Ivy picked up the thread. "But you broke through all of that. And knowing what I do now, I think you're maybe the only one who could shake him out of that inertia."

"Me? Why?"

"There's this whole transition period when you get out of military service," Harrison explained, "trying to figure out how the hell to be part of the civilian world. We've all been through some measure of it, wondering where we fit. For Rangers in particular, we're accustomed to being part of a tight team, to knowing those men have our six. Being out, without that backup, it's easy to feel kind of adrift, even when leaving was a choice. With Garrett and Ty being a unit well before they joined up, his has just been a thousand times worse."

"Without his best friend as a reference point, Ty doesn't remember who he is. It's helped, him moving here to be near Harrison and Sebastian, but it's not the same. You, though. You were part of his life before the Army. Arguably the biggest part other than Garrett. Your very presence reminds him of how to be him. That history, those patterns you established years ago, back when he was still happy, remind him that he *can* still be happy. I can't begin to tell you how thrilled I am that his feelings for you are strong enough to overcome the survivor's guilt and the idea that he doesn't deserve to be."

Why did the idea of that feel like a suffocating pressure? "I don't even know what to say to that."

Harrison studied her. "For what it's worth, Garrett never stopped giving him shit for letting you go. Every time we were stateside, he tried to get Ty to look you up. Ty insisted you were better off without him. He never used your name, or I'd have put two and two together when I met you."

What would she have done if he'd come back to her on his own, not as a matter of chance? Paisley didn't know. She'd had fantasies of exactly that for years. In some of them, she'd let the hurt win and turned him away, but knowing how she'd felt when she'd seen him in that reception hall, as if the world that had stopped spinning the day he'd gotten on that bus for basic training had started up again, in all likelihood, she'd have thrown herself willingly into his arms and whatever relationship he'd have given her. Exactly as she'd done now. But if it had been before he'd gotten out, she might have lost him all over again to Garrett's death. Or worse, to death in combat as he'd always feared.

But despite Ivy and Harrison's enthusiastic support of her relationship with Ty, she didn't know how to trust it. Not with the same no-holds-barred abandon she had as a teenager. They both had a lot more baggage, and she was afraid of the ghosts that lurked within it. Because, despite her inherent romanticism, she knew that outside of books, love didn't always conquer all.

"I APPRECIATE YOUR COOPERATION." The words had become rote for Ty over the past few days.

"No problem. I hope you get to the bottom of it soon. Tell Paisley I said hi."

"I will." Ty hung up on Dustin Phelps, a college baseball coach who now lived in Texas.

That was it. He'd officially cleared everybody on Paisley's list, and he was no closer to figuring out who was harassing her than he had been when he'd started this. The theory that had felt so promising in the beginning wasn't panning out, and there had been no further incidents since they got back to Eden's Ridge. Not entirely surprising. Presumably her stalker had a job of some kind back in the Nashville area that would preclude a lot of trips four hours away. It didn't mean this was over.

After sending Paisley a quick text to let her know he was on his way home, he turned the details over in his head, looking for a new angle. He couldn't shake the idea that it was someone who knew her offline somehow. There were gifts sent that couldn't have been parsed out from her social media accounts or the newsletters she'd sent. Someone *knew* her somehow. The question was who and from where? Paisley was a social creature. She knew lots of people from lots of places, and that didn't rule out some kind of secondary connection between the stalker and someone who *did* know her well and might have inadvertently shared more about her than they'd realized. None of that narrowed the scope of the investigation. He needed another thread to tug.

She'd left lights on, he noted. It wasn't something he normally bothered with, but he found he appreciated how that small thing made the cabin feel warm and welcoming against the chill winter air. More homey. Everything about having her here made the place feel more like a home than just a place he'd been parking his ass for more than a year. What would it be like to do this for real? To share a house, a life, with her? That wasn't a fantasy he'd let himself entertain for what felt like an eon. But stepping inside, seeing all the little touches she'd added, all the signs of cohabitation and her sweet, silly dog, it was hard not to think about it.

A car pulled up outside. A minute later, Paisley swung through the door, bags in her hands, Duke on her heels. "I have dinner fixin's."

Because he was still thinking about that fantasy, Ty crossed to her, curling his hands around the bags and bringing his lips to hers. She softened, leaning into him in that moment of surrender he craved. Some of those sharp edges he'd lived with for so long smoothed out a little. "Hi."

"Hi to you, too."

They grinned at each other for a moment before Ty remembered the groceries. He tugged them from her hands and carried them over to the kitchen. "How was your day?"

"More productive. The book is finally starting to gain some momentum again. And I spent some time this afternoon helping Harrison brainstorm a social media campaign for his next release. How about you?"

"Less fun. Between patrols and calls, I finished chasing down the last of your exes."

"Oh?" He heard the instant tension in her voice and hated it.

"Dead end. You are apparently the only woman in history to actually end on legitimately good terms with all your exes. Even the ones you've lost touch with were incredibly complimentary of you and concerned about the situation." She'd been consistently described as warm and fun. To a man, they'd all wished her well and offered to help if they could. "They basically collectively all said hi."

She blew out a breath. "Well, I can't say that doesn't make me feel better. I'd like to think I'm a good judge of character. I haven't ever dated anyone I didn't think was a good person."

"Seems your record is safe, and my investigation is at a roadblock."

"I know this means we'll have to poke around some other area of my life, but can we just give it a rest for the night? I'd like to cook dinner for us and just...chill."

"We can do that." Tucking away the nagging thoughts that had circled for days, he watched as she began unloading groceries. "What are we having?"

"Spatchcocked chicken and roasted vegetables."

"You're making that up. It's some kind of romance writer dick joke, right?"

Her smile flashed. "While I'm more than capable of making a dirty joke about basically anything, I swear it's a real thing. Google it. You'll see. It's just the name for the technique where you cut the spine out of a whole chicken and press it flat, so it cooks faster. Makes roast chicken more possible for a weeknight dinner that way."

"Riiiiight."

She handed over a bottle of wine. "Here, make yourself useful and open this."

"Yes ma'am."

He uncorked the wine and poured them both a glass as she turned on the oven to preheat and began prepping vegetables. She kept up a running conversation about inconsequential, everyday things. Normal. It was both surreal and wonderful, and Ty let himself bask in it, enjoying her. Then she reached into the cabinet for some olive oil, and something white fluttered to the floor, destroying his domestic fantasy like the screech of a record.

For a moment, he was paralyzed, unsure if he should lunge for the invitation—which would make it a Thing—or ignore it. His heart beat thick in his throat, full of dread and a need to *act* against a threat he couldn't fully articulate.

Paisley picked up the card and set it aside, moving back to the vegetables with the oil. "You like parsnips, right?"

He exhaled a slow, controlled breath, working to level his system. "I don't know if I've ever had them. Aren't they basically just white carrots?"

"No. They're sweet when roasted but a little sharper. I like them for something different, and they'll taste divine with the pan sauce from the chicken."

Ty edged behind her, dropping a kiss to the juncture of her neck and shoulder as a distraction as he reached for the invitation.

"You really need to give Bethany an answer, even if it's to decline."

His hand froze and the world narrowed. One moment ticked into four before he found his voice. "You've already seen it?"

"Yeah."

Why should that easy answer make him feel so exposed? She'd probably found it when cooking something else since she'd been here. "Why didn't you say anything?"

"I didn't think it was my place."

"And now it is?" He stepped away from her,

knowing his voice was too hard, too sharp, but he couldn't seem to stop it. She was shining a light on his biggest wound, and it made him want to lash out. That shit belonged to the dark.

Paisley turned, the easy humor gone from her face. "You made it my place when you changed the rules. You said it yourself—we aren't ever going to be casual. This relationship extends beyond the bedroom, Galahad. You've just spent the last several days going over my life with a fine-toothed comb, but I know very little of yours."

There was truth to what she was saying. And Ty was willing to tell her almost anything. Anything but this.

She reached out, laying a tentative hand on his arm. "I know this is one of those things you said will never heal. I'm not trying to get you to slice open a vein here, but if we're going to make it this time, I need more than these carefully curated pieces of you."

"That's not what I'm doing." That made it sound like it was deliberate and about her. He didn't talk about this with anyone.

"We each had a life the last eighteen years. You can't just redact all of yours."

God, there were days when he wished he could. How much better would it feel to wipe out the memories that haunted him? Even as he thought it, the guilt spewed up, clogging his throat. Wiping out the memories would be to wipe out Garrett. Memories were the only thing he had left. And she wanted him to trot that shit out for conversation? "You don't know what you're asking."

"I think I do. I'm not here to force you into reliving the trauma. I don't need to know all the details. But I'm not some stranger or a well-meaning shrink. I knew Garrett. I know what he meant to you. And I know that his death is eating you alive. You've been losing yourself in my case, in me. But I see it underneath, and I'm afraid if we don't acknowledge the ghost in the room, it's going to fester until it becomes something we can't survive."

He didn't know how to acknowledge that ghost without falling back into darkness. He'd worked too damned hard to claw his way back out to risk that again. To risk taking her down with him.

She stepped closer, cupping his cheek. "I don't want to lose you because we can't talk to each other. You believing that you couldn't did not end well for us before."

Ty closed his eyes at the old pain in her voice. He hadn't known how to talk to her about his choice to go into the Army. And there'd been a big part of him that had held back because she'd had the power to change his mind. But he knew the silence had hurt her almost as much as the breaking up. Because she'd believed they'd shared almost everything. Why should that have changed for her?

Ty opened his eyes, taking in the expression of earnest yearning in her face. She wanted so desperately for him to trust her, to give her this piece of himself. He could see, too, the underlying expectation that he wouldn't, and in that doubt, he recognized the seed of their destruction. She needed more than surface. He'd known that, hadn't he? It was why he'd tried—poorly—to resist the siren song of what she offered. But he'd thought they'd have more time.

It was hardly the first time he'd been wrong on that front. Time was a precious and fickle commodity. It seemed theirs was up.

She couldn't possibly understand that in asking him to open this wound, he'd absolutely destroy her view of him as a hero. But he didn't deserve to have her keep looking at him like that. It wasn't who he was, and she needed to know the hot mess she was taking on before they got in any deeper. He'd promised himself he'd do right by her. Maybe it would be better for her this way.

He'd have preferred going through Ranger School again with one arm tied behind his back than talking about any of this shit. He didn't know how to handle the grief in any other way besides ignoring it or channeling it into something else. He'd given up trying to drown it after Harrison stopped him from taking the coward's way out. Running from this, shoving it under the bed like a corpse, was just another step down the coward's path. He might be a failure, but he wasn't a coward.

"We were in a convoy." The words were like razors in his throat. "Doesn't matter where or why. It was a typical part of the job. Typical day. We were a little over a month into our deployment, settling into the rhythm, such as it was. Garrett was hyped. He'd just had a video call with Bethany, which always pumped him up, but this was more than usual. I finally asked him what the hell was going on, and he says it's time for him to think about getting out. It wasn't like we hadn't talked about it before, when things got really bad. But we'd both ultimately decided we'd put in our twenty years first, so this felt out of left field."

Because his legs didn't feel altogether steady, Ty slumped back against the counter. "I asked him why the change of heart. He's all but bouncing in his seat like a kid with a secret. Says he's not supposed to tell, but who the hell am I gonna blab to on the other side of the world? With the biggest smile I've ever seen on him, he tells me Bethany's pregnant. And then the fucking world blew up."

He closed his eyes again, seeing the dust and the blood. Christ, the blood.

Paisley's hands wrapped around his, an anchor that pulled him back to the now. He wanted to feel all of her, to lose himself exactly as she'd accused him of doing, but he needed to get through this, so he focused on the warmth of her grip and breathed through the grief shredding his chest.

"Our Hummer had hit a roadside bomb. We were taking on fire. Most of the convoy was already dead by the time I managed to find Garrett. He'd been thrown from the wreckage, and he'd—" Ty swallowed. "His leg was gone."

Paisley made a small, choked noise, but said nothing.

"I managed to get him to cover, get a tourniquet on. I don't know how long it took for backup to arrive. It felt like years. And the whole time, I'm returning enemy fire, swearing and shouting at him to just keep fucking hanging on. Then the helo set down, and I thought, thank God. The flight doctor started work on him the second we lifted off, and the medic was shoving me down to deal with shrapnel in my shoulder I hadn't even noticed. Then he was just...gone. No last words. No nothing. Just...gone."

Ty could still see Garrett's limp arm slipping off the stretcher before the drugs took him under. "I swore to protect him, and I failed."

"You did everything you could. You didn't plant that IED."

So, he'd been told, over and over. On his good days, he believed it, a little.

"No. But it was supposed to be me in that seat. It should've been me who died. He should have been able to go home to his wife and child like I promised Bethany he would the day they got married." His throat closed up on the words as he fought back the tide of emotion.

"That wasn't a reasonable promise."

Ty stiffened, starting to pull away, but Paisley held on, her expression fierce.

"No, listen to me. You were brothers. There isn't a soul who knew the two of you who didn't understand that. You were both willing to lay your lives on the line for each other. And you did that, over and over again. But you aren't God. Garrett died because of circumstances outside your control, not because you somehow shirked your duty to protect him."

His throat burned with unshed tears as he uttered the truth he'd told no one else. "I couldn't protect her either. She lost the baby." And the last piece of his best friend had died with it.

"Oh, Ty." Paisley cradled his face, and there was no pity in her eyes. Neither was there disappointment. Only a profound sharing of his grief that he didn't know how to accept. She pressed against him, wrapping him in an embrace he understood was meant to banish his demons.

"I can't face her. I can't do it knowing she lost everything because I couldn't keep him safe."

"Okay." She held tighter, brushing a soft kiss to his jaw. "Okay."

And after an eternity warring with himself, Ty let himself lean on her and wept.

11

Paisley woke late, instinctively reaching for Ty. But his side of the bed was empty and cold. The scent of coffee told her he was already up. No sound of movement or jangle of dog tags came from below, so he'd probably taken Duke out for a walk. Collapsing back on her pillow, she wondered for a moment if she'd dreamed last night.

For the first time since she'd begun sharing his bed, Ty had woken her with a nightmare, shouting for Garrett. Her fault. When she'd managed to pull him out of it, she'd thought he'd turn away, get up to pace off all that adrenaline. Instead, he'd turned to her, losing himself in her body, as if he could cleanse his mind with the fire of passion. She shifted at the memory, and a sufficient number of aches proved that, at least, hadn't been a dream. She'd held him after, until they'd both slid back into sleep.

Where did they stand now? Was him being up and going already this morning just his usual morning-person inability to stay in bed? Or was he putting distance between them? She wished she knew. Before last night, she'd based most of her decisions around what she knew of the boy she'd loved beyond reason. There was still plenty of him in the man, but this was uncharted territory, and she hadn't figured out how to navigate the space between who he'd been and who he was now.

The door opened, and Duke's paws clicked on the hardwood as he pranced inside. Paisley rolled out of bed, grabbing a robe before making her way downstairs. Ty was already dressed for his workday.

As she hit the first floor, her dog bounded over with a happy yip.

Ty glanced at them, his expression neutral. "There's coffee."

She rubbed Duke down with hands that trembled from nerves. "Thanks."

All business, Ty looped the leash on a hook. "He's had some exercise and emptied both tanks, so he should be good to go." Before she could figure out what to say, he was buckling on his duty belt. "I have a briefing, so I have to go in a bit early."

"Oh. Okay." *Lame. Inadequate.* But she had nothing to work with here. No proper cues to act off of.

A frown finally cracked the neutrality. "I don't like leaving you alone."

But he wanted out of this house, away from her. It was clear in all his body language.

Fighting to keep her own face neutral, she buried her hands in Duke's fur. "I'll be fine. I'll just grab a shower and get on over to Ivy and Harrison's." Not that she was in a hurry. While her friends had been marvelously accommodating, she was beginning to feel like an imposition and wanted some silence and empty space to think about the murky middle of this book. Not that she'd be thinking about that now.

Taking her at her word, he nodded sharply, draining the contents from a mug on the counter before setting it in the sink and starting for the door. "Lock the door and set the alarm behind me."

She absorbed the inherent rejection in the gesture, managing only a monosyllabic, "Okay."

She'd hold herself together until he left. In just a few more moments, he'd be out the door, and she could flagellate herself for how badly she'd screwed things up by pushing him.

Ty paused, one hand on the knob. "I'm sorry. I'm trying to get my head on straight."

"I'm sorry I pushed you."

"You were right. We won't last without honesty. I'm just struggling." He hesitated, as if he was going to say something else.

Look at me. She willed him to turn around. To come back to touch her.

But he only opened the door. "I'll see you tonight."

The latch snicked quietly into place. Because she knew he was waiting on the other side, she threw the deadbolt and set the alarm to stay. Booted footsteps trotted down the stairs, and a moment later his cruiser was backing out of the driveway. Then he was gone.

She needed coffee and some alone time to get her own head on straight and decide whether she'd allow this knot of tears in her throat to actually dissolve or not. Pouring a cup into the insulated mug Ty had so thoughtfully packed for her, she sank onto the sofa, patting her lap in invitation. Duke leaped up, assuming his favorite position for cuddles and belly scratches.

That had gone both better and worse than she expected. She'd wanted him to open up to her, but what was the cost? Had she damaged this nascent thing between them by forcing the issue? Should she have ignored the invitation, as he had? Stuck with the plan for a quiet night to chill? She'd needed to know where his head was. That he was drowning survivor's guilt was no surprise. Blaming himself for Garrett, for Bethany's unborn child, was illogical. But nothing about this was based on logic. That wasn't how trauma worked. And his was still so very close to the surface.

She wanted to help him. She wanted to heal him. But despite Ivy's confidence, Paisley didn't know if she could, or if he'd even let her.

"He said he was struggling. Admitting it has to mean something, right?"

Duke nudged the hand that had stopped back into motion on his chest.

"Last night was a lot. Obviously, it brought up some stuff again. It's totally reasonable that he needs space after that. He's been carrying this around on his own for a long time. It doesn't mean he's going to shut me out completely."

She decided to take Duke's sneeze of pleasure as agreement.

Because the knot was still in her throat, she lingered over coffee and pupper snuggles until it had shrunk to a more manageable level.

"Shower time, pal. Then we're gonna go see our buddies. Okay?"

At the word "go", Duke bounced up, ready for action, tail making a helicopter motion.

"You gotta wait. Let's get you a puzzle while mama showers."

Paisley set him up, then dug out the little Bluetooth speaker Ty had packed. Some nice, upbeat music would perk her up so she hopefully didn't get an immediate interrogation once she got to Ivy's. By the time her Pick-Me-Up playlist rolled through Pharrell Williams' "Happy" and Michael Bublé's "I've Got the World on a String", past "Uptown Funk" and on into Fleetwood Mac's "Don't Stop", she was feeling more positive. And of course, when Queen's "Bohemian Rhapsody" came on, she had to join in. Because obviously.

From outside the bathroom Duke began to bark.

"Your opinion on my vocal stylings is not called for, little man!"

He piped down, and she finished her shower

in relative peace. Wrapping herself in a towel, she stepped out, waving away the cloud of steam. The bright pop of color on the kitchen island had her stopping in her tracks. A profusion of Gerbera daisies, purple tulips, and vibrant Asiatic lilies burst from a vase in the center.

Tears sprung to her eyes again as she spun, looking for Ty. But he'd apparently been running some kind of covert op to sneak in and deliver these and get back out again for work. He'd probably expected her to already be gone. Crossing over, she picked up the card leaning against the vase and slipped it free of the tiny envelope.

I've never felt closer to anyone.

Oh, sweet, sweet man. He'd understood she needed some reassurance after their rocky morning. As apologies went, this knocked it out of the park.

She started to call him but, just in case that briefing he'd mentioned was actually happening, switched to a text instead.

Paisley: **You are a sweet, sneaky man. Thank you for the flowers!**

The dot bubble popped up as he typed his reply.

What flowers?

Rolling her eyes at his attempt to play innocent, she snapped a photo and sent it.

The phone rang almost immediately. Ty, of course.

She was smiling as she answered. "That was a really sweet surprise for when I got out of the shower."

"Paisley, I didn't leave you flowers. I've been in this briefing for the last forty-five minutes."

"What? Then wh—" Slowly, she turned from the flowers to look at the alarm panel across the room.

It wasn't lit. She *knew* she'd set it.

Skin crawling with gooseflesh, she whirled, looking frantically to see if someone was still there. But there was nowhere to hide except the loft. Duke seemed unperturbed...but he'd been barking.

"Someone's been in the house. While I was *in the shower!*" she hissed.

"I'm coming home."

"Hurry."

"Stay on the line."

She heard him speaking to someone else then sounds of hurried footsteps and the slam of a car door.

Clothes. She needed clothes. She didn't dare

go up to the loft in case some kind of boogie man was hiding under the bed, so she rummaged through the laundry waiting in the tiny, stacked dryer, hauling out one of Ty's multitude of flannel shirts and some sweatpants and yanking them on.

He'd been here. She was no longer able to think of this threat as anything but male. He'd been here, *in the house*, while she was naked in the shower. Her dog had barked at him, and she'd been blissfully unaware while she sang those stupid songs.

What if he'd come in the bathroom? What if he'd trapped her there, while she was at her most vulnerable? What if he'd had a weapon? Her writer's mind spun with scenarios, each more horrific and terrifying than the last. What if? What if? What if?

Duke whined, clearly picking up on her distress. He nudged at her hand.

"You still there?" Ty demanded.

"Yeah. Yeah, I'm here."

"We're coming, okay? We're coming."

She grabbed a cast-iron skillet off the row of hooks on the wall and backed into a corner with her dog to wait.

～

As a Ranger, Ty had nearly two decades of training and experience in how to compartmentalize and push through fear for the sake of a mission. He had to draw on all of it as he drove like a bat out of hell, with Paisley's unsteady breath on the other end of the phone.

Why the fuck had he chosen to live so far out? Why had he left her alone this morning? She had no protection. He knew damned well Duke was worthless as a guard dog. It was too easy to imagine someone holding her at gunpoint or with a knife to her throat, threatening her to stay quiet.

Because the questions and the multitude of dangerous scenarios ate away at his focus, he locked them away with the fear, too. Something to bring out once she was safe and the perimeter was secure. He ran lights on, siren screaming, coaxing every ounce of speed out of the cruiser's engine as he clung to curves.

"Still with me, baby?"

"Yeah." Her voice was too small, too quiet. Soft enough he could hear Duke's agitated panting.

"I'm nearly there."

"I can hear the sirens."

Let the bastard know he was coming. He'd rather run the threat off than risk Paisley getting hurt. The part of his brain still capable of rational thought recognized that she was probably safe. The flowers were meant to scare her, but there'd still been no direct contact. At most, the fucker was hiding in the woods watching, maybe getting off on watching them scurry like ants.

But he could feel the pulse of her fear over the phone, and that overrode everything else, lighting up a primitive part of his brain that didn't give a shit about anything but getting to her as fast as humanly possible. He fishtailed into the driveway and skidded to a stop, not caring that he sprayed his own truck with gravel in the process. Urgency beat in his blood, driving him out of the car, up the steps, gun drawn.

Training kept him from just barging in with no cover. Years of habit had him following protocol, getting through the door to clear the room. It was that muscle memory that kept him from being koshed over the head. He pivoted, and something heavy and black glanced off his shoulder as he brought up his weapon.

Paisley dropped...was that a cast-iron skillet? "Ty!"

He barely had time to holster his gun before she threw herself at him. Absorbing her momentum, he wrapped her tight, still visually clearing the room, checking for threats. It wasn't until there was no enemy fire that he fully let go of the idea that this wasn't some kind of trap.

Outside he could hear the rest of his backup arrive. Car doors slammed. Xander shouted, "Fan out!"

But Ty's focus narrowed in on Paisley.

He'd burst in on countless civilians in various war-torn countries. Everyday citizens just trying to survive, never knowing when violence would rear its head. Women and children huddling in silent terror, waiting for the end. Ty had expected something of that in her eyes. And there was fear when he pulled back to search her pale face. But there was equal part fury.

That he'd left her alone? That he'd broken yet another promise? That he wasn't the protector he'd set himself up to be?

Yeah, he deserved her anger for that and more. But there'd be time for recriminations later. "Are you hurt?"

She gave a quick, sharp shake of her head. "I know I should've been gone already, but I got caught up and I just...I wasn't expecting...this."

"Of course, you weren't. This asshole is getting bolder." Which begged the question...what would be the next step?

Xander, Clyde, and Leanne came in.

"No sign of anybody." Xander nodded to Paisley. "You must be Miss Parish. I'm Sheriff Kincaid. This is Deputy Parker and County Investigator Leanne Hammond. Sorry for the trouble. Can you tell us exactly what happened?"

Sucking in a breath, she stepped away from Ty, reaching automatically for Duke. "Ty left for work about seven fifteen. I locked the door and set the alarm before he even pulled out of the driveway. I've been spending my days with Ivy and Harrison Wilkes for the past week, so I was getting ready to head that way, but I just wanted to linger over my coffee a while."

Xander flashed a reassuring smile. "Best way to enjoy coffee. Go on."

She took them through it. As she talked about the realization that Ty hadn't sent the flowers and that the alarm was no longer on, she shook harder, her fingers fisting in the dog's ruff. Here was the fear that righteous anger had drowned out. She didn't look at Ty as she spoke, and he felt the greasy fingers of guilt slithering through him.

"Was the door locked when you got here?" Xander asked.

Ty crossed his arms so he wouldn't give in to the urge to curl his hands into fists. "No. She about took off my head with the skillet though."

Clyde picked it up off the floor, testing the heft. "Good choice."

Leanne snapped a picture of the flowers. "I'm gonna try to get up with Misty. See if she sold any in the last couple days that would fit this description."

"Good." Xander nodded in approval. "Brooks, let's check out this alarm system, see what happened there."

"Can...can one of you check the loft?" Paisley asked.

"On it!" Clyde trotted over, and Ty dutifully followed Xander outside.

It only took minutes to find the cut phone line.

"Older system. Came with the place when Porter bought it. Reckon he'll be upgrading now."

Ty grunted. He should have updated it himself. Should have beefed up his own security, as he had Paisley's house in Nashville. But he'd been arrogant, figuring he and his training would make up the difference. The more fool him. "It's not that sophisticated a system, but it still indicates we're dealing with someone who has some kind of knowledge."

"You suspected that when you searched her house, though, right?"

"More in a staying open to all possibilities kind

of way. The Metro PD detective on the case thought I was a paranoid nut job."

"Not looking so paranoid now. Good instincts."

Ty wasn't sure his instincts could be trusted.

"Hey, Brooks? You okay?"

"The woman I'm supposed to protect just had a home invasion while she was in the shower. What do you think?"

Unruffled, Xander clapped him on the shoulder. "Put it away, man. That kind of thinking will run you crazy, and you're no good to her like that."

He wasn't sure he was any good to her as it was.

"You have access to monitor the system you set up in Nashville?"

"Yeah."

"Check it. See if anybody's been screwing with that."

But all systems appeared to be functioning normally. No recordings, no interference, no alarms. Which would make sense since her stalker was here instead of there.

"Maybe Leanne has something."

Back inside, Paisley was coming out of the bathroom, dressed in her own clothes. Her eyes met Ty's and held for a few, unreadable beats before she looked away again. A little bit of color had come back into her cheeks, but she still seemed a little shaky.

"Misty hasn't sold anything like this at any point in the last two weeks," Leanne reported. "The flowers didn't come from Moonbeams and Sweet Dreams. We can try checking with florists in surrounding towns, but that might take a while."

"The stalker's in the Nashville area," Paisley said. "They could've come from there, in which case, you'll never manage to track the purchase."

Which left them where? Still no real leads to follow, no closer to an answer, with yet another space that should have been safe violated.

This bastard was mocking him. Or that was what it felt like.

She's not safe with you.

Short of sequestering them both in a remote location under 24-hour guard—which even Ty recognized was not the answer—he was running out of options, and he was beginning to doubt his ability to figure it out.

"Pack your stuff. We're not staying here."

A frisson of irritation flickered over her features. Probably about the bossy thing. She could deal.

"Where are we going?"

"I don't know yet."

"There's space up at the inn," Xander put in. "Lots of people around. I'll call my wife, get her to book you in."

Ty nodded. That would work until he could make a better plan. "Appreciate it."

With a sigh, Paisley turned away and began to gather her things. Again.

12

"Do you want to tell me why I had to hear from my sister-in-law that you and Ty have moved into the inn?"

Paisley scowled at Emerson's voice on the phone, wondering which one of Caleb's four sisters had blabbed. Either Xander's wife, Kennedy, or Pru, the one who also had a teenage daughter. "Hello to you too, Em. How are things in preggoland?"

"Don't change the subject. What's going on?"

Probably Pru.

Knowing she'd been cornered, Paisley shoved back from the desk and began to pace the confines of the comfortable room that had begun to feel like a prison over the past three days. "That little maybe-a-stalker problem has turned into definitely-a-stalker problem." She gave Emerson the summarized version of events as Duke trailed her around the room like a faithful shadow.

"Oh my God! Why didn't you tell me?

"I didn't want to worry you."

"How bad is it?"

"I mean, I've been forced to uproot again. Without being consulted. Again." She sighed. "On top of which, I'm beyond tired of having my life interrupted. All this chaos isn't conducive to my work. Your sisters-in-law are lovely, and the inn is great, but I'm desperate for some privacy and routine."

A deep male voice spoke up. "I have another brother who can help with that."

Of course, Caleb was right there. His seemingly endless parade of former foster siblings was the epitome of "I've got a guy for that."

"Hi, Caleb. And that's not necessary."

"Are you sure you're safe there?" Emerson asked. "I mean, Ty still has to work, right? He's not on 24-hour bodyguard duty?"

"No, he's not. But I'm as safe here as anywhere. It's a houseful of people."

"Offer stands."

"Thanks." She paused. "Is Caleb still right there?"

"He doesn't have to be."

"Understood. Girl talk. I'm gonna go take Mooch for a run. Take care, Pais. Be careful."

"I will."

"Okay, he's gone. What is it, babe?"

"I'm worried about Ty. When this started, it felt like we were a team in this, but since this latest thing, he's been in a really bad headspace. We've slept in the same bed, but he's barely touched me. He's not really sleeping, and I can sense him spiraling. He's been all up in his head and is spending long hours chasing...well, I have no idea what leads because he's not talking to me. He's shutting me out, and I don't know what to do about it."

"That's a tough one. He promised you'd be safe, and then you weren't. That's got to mess with his whole alpha-male-protector view of himself."

"I don't blame him for that."

"Yeah, but it sounds like he does. Maybe he needs a confidence boost. Something to remind him that you still see him as capable."

"Maybe." But Paisley didn't think it would be anywhere near that simple.

The door opened, and Ty strode in, walking straight by her, into the bathroom.

"I gotta go. Ty just got back. Give my love to, Fi."

"Will do. Good luck."

Hanging up, Paisley tossed her phone on the bed.

The shower started up. Maybe she could join him and get past this wall that had grown up between them. But when she tried the knob, it was locked. Resigned to waiting, she considered going back to the book, but everything she'd written the last few days had been tossed.

When he emerged half an hour later, he didn't look any more relaxed. The strain of the last days showed on his face, in the tense line of his jaw. Needing to do something to soothe, Paisley crossed the room, wrapping her arms around him, not caring that the damp from his shower was soaking her shirt. But he stepped away, moving to the duffel bag with his clothes.

Trying not to take offense, she dropped into the desk chair. "Talk to me, Galahad."

He flinched. "Don't call me that."

"I've always called you that."

With fast, jerky movements, he began to dress. "I'm no knight."

Duke whined and nose bumped Ty's hip. He ignored the dog, too.

"I mean, right now you're acting more like the Dark one, but Bruce Wayne is a mouthful, and I don't think I can call you Batman with a straight face."

The attempt at humor fell as flat as the expression in his hazel eyes. "You can really joke right now?"

"When I think you're being ridiculous, yes." God knew, if she took this too seriously right now, she was probably going to break down. "It's a nickname, Ty. One I've used for years that you always used to like."

A muscle jumped in his jaw as he yanked a shirt over his head. "I'm not who I used to be."

"Yes, you are. You're still my personal hero."

"How can you honestly look at me and say that?"

Confidence boost. Right, I can endure some embarrassment if it'll help him get through this.

"Because it's how I've always I've seen you. Every male lead I imagined for my books was another incarnation of you. Different features, different professions, different situations, but still, at the heart, the man I've always seen."

With a look of profound disgust, he shook his

head. "Then you're blinded by your own romanticism. Wake up to fucking reality, Paisley. The world isn't handing out happy endings. Life isn't some fairy tale, and I'm not like the ridiculous heroes in your books. I don't have the answers. I don't even know the right goddamn questions anymore. I couldn't save Garrett, and I'm never going to save you, so stop putting that on me!"

His words hung in the air between them like poison gas. Paisley couldn't speak past the stunning pain as they leeched into her. As the silence turned long and toxic, Ty jammed his feet into boots, grabbed his keys, and walked out the door, slamming it behind him.

Paisley sank down on the bed already feeling the tears coursing down her cheeks. Duke slunk over, tail tucked, and wriggled his way under her arm. Pressing her face into his fur, she held her sweet, loyal dog, and wept.

Rationally, she recognized that Ty was lashing out, taking out his frustrated impotence at the situation on her. But she was hurting too, damn it. He'd just essentially reduced her to a silly schoolgirl, one without a single toe in reality. She could take being there for his healing, if he was going to heal, but not if he was going to dismiss her life's work. Not once, in any of her many many relationships had she tolerated a lack of respect. She wasn't about to start now.

He wanted to be free of her expectation that he'd save her. The expectation she'd never explicitly put on him. Fine. She'd leave and lift that burden. She'd been leaving all her life, hadn't she? Running was what she knew best. She'd believed for years that men could be enjoyed but not counted on. He was the whole reason for that belief. Shame on her for believing he'd changed.

Grabbing her phone, she tapped a text to Emerson.

Talk to Caleb's brother.

TY EYED his fourth shot of whiskey.

This was a bad idea. But, hell, he was full of bad ideas. Like starting things back up with Paisley. Like believing he could protect her. Like thinking he could ever possibly deserve to have her look at him as a hero.

Terrible ideas across the board.

Oh, and he couldn't forget to add being an insecure asshole and yelling at the woman he loved and essentially calling her stupid for thinking he was anything other than the miserable, broken sack of shit he was.

Remembering the stunned devastation on her face, he picked up the glass and tossed it back. The shot burned its way down his gullet, but the whiskey didn't burn nearly as bad as the shame. By his recollection, he needed the rest of the bottle to outrun that. Maybe more. A sketchy place like The Right Attitude probably watered down their drinks. But where else was a man going to drink himself blind on alcohol that could probably double as paint stripper? Home? No, he didn't dare go back there. Not when he knew he'd see Paisley's absence in every square inch of the place. He'd probably have to move.

Before he could lift his hand to signal the bartender for another, a familiar figure slid onto the stool beside him. Harrison eyed the row of empty glasses. "Thought you gave this up."

Instead of answering the implied question, Ty asked one of his own. "How did you find me?"

"We split up. Sebastian headed out to your place. Porter took the tavern. I was the lucky winner."

"How'd you even know to look for me?"

"Your, shall we say, precipitous exit from the inn did not go unnoticed. Ari texted Ivy."

Ty squinted through eyes that were starting to go a little bleary, trying to place the name. Dark hair. High school student. Thought Paisley was the coolest thing since...something cool. "Why does Pru and Flynn's teenage daughter even have Ivy's number?"

"They became buds when Ivy stayed there last year. Anyway, she indicated that you and Paisley had a fight, and you did not look great when you left. Given the state of the investigation and the fact you've been wound tighter than a bow string for days, it seemed prudent to check." He glanced at the glasses again. "You planning on keeping going with that?"

"You planning to stop me?"

"From getting behind the wheel, absolutely, but if you want to get shit-faced instead of actually dealing with the problem, that's your call." He shrugged, as if it truly didn't matter to him. "It's a dumb call, but your life, such as it is."

Bristling, Ty curled his fingers around the empty glass instead of into a fist. He'd clocked Harrison once over hard truths and had felt like an asshole ever since. Even in this state, he wouldn't do it again.

"I fucked everything up, just like I knew I would. I hurt her, just like before. Except this time, it wasn't because I had some noble purpose, but because I'm too fucking broken to be what she needs and deserves."

The bartender wandered back over, pointing at the bottle that would bring him oblivion for just a little while, but at a shake of Harrison's head, he retreated again.

"What exactly do you think that is?"

"Somebody who can be that hero she's always wanted. Somebody who can keep her safe and find this asshole who's upending her life. Somebody who doesn't make promises he can't keep."

"Hm." Harrison glanced at his watch. "Should've been Sebastian to catch you in this mood."

"What the hell is that supposed to mean?"

"Just that he's got a lot more experience shoveling horse shit."

"Excuse me?"

"That is some grade-A, top-quality horse shit, my brother. And maybe that's on me. I'm the one who told you last year you needed to find a new mission. I didn't realize you'd take me quite so literally."

"What are you talking about?"

"Finding a new mission is not about taking that literal military mission mentality and applying it to everything else. You've been treating life like a fucking op. One with an expiration date any day now. You haven't set down roots, haven't connected with anybody but those already in your inner circle. Until Paisley. She snuck past that infamous guard of yours because she was already there. And it's been the best damned thing that could have happened to you. Over the past weeks, I've seen you alive again, not just going through the motions. But you've turned *her* into a mission, and that's not how love works. She's a person. A pretty damned awesome one. She is not with you because she needs or wants a bodyguard. She's with you because she loves you. It's in every look, every word she writes. That's not a thing you have to earn. It's a gift, and to act like it's anything else is the height of foolishness."

He hadn't been treating life like a mission. He'd just been surviving, existing until she came back into his life. She'd made him want to be that hero she claimed to see. He'd tried. He'd tried so damned hard to live up to those expectations. To be worthy of her love. And he'd failed.

"I didn't protect her."

"You're running an op without enough information. Sometimes shit gets FUBAR. You know that. But she's fine. She's safe. And if you'll pull your head out of your ass, you'll keep her that way." He laid a hand on Ty's shoulder. "Don't throw her away because you're conflating your feelings about Garrett's death with this situation. You're not responsible for the actions of other people. You're only responsible for your own."

His own actions had likely destroyed whatever chance he'd had with Paisley. "I was an asshole."

"I'm sure you were. Just as I'm sure she'll forgive you for it once you've appropriately groveled."

Something ballooned in his chest. It took him a minute to recognize it for what it was. Hope.

Was Harrison right? Did he stand a chance of having her forgive him even after everything he'd said, all the pulling away and hot and cold routine? Only one way to find out. Ty dug out his wallet and threw money on the bar. As he slid off the stool, the room promptly dipped.

Harrison's arm slipped around him. "Whoa there. Gotcha."

"I need to go apologize for all the things." And then maybe he could underscore all of those apologies with orgasms. She liked those. Maybe *that* was his new mission. Seemed like a way better one than what he'd been on.

Harrison began to steer him across the scarred wood floor toward the door. "I think you need to sober up first. I'm not gonna dump your ass on Paisley to take care of in this condition. We're going back to my place so you can sleep it off."

"We can brainstorm how I should grovel."

He tugged open the door. "I'm sure Ivy will be full of ideas."

13

Paisley went from sleep to wakefulness in an instant, knowing even before she reached for the other side of the bed that the warm presence there was Duke instead of Ty.

He hadn't come back after storming out last night.

Maybe she shouldn't have expected him to, but she'd gotten a brief text from Harrison saying that he was safe, and she'd thought, once he had a chance to calm down, he'd work his way around to apologizing. Or, at the very least, showing up for guard duty. He was the one so determined that she needed a bodyguard.

But he hadn't used those stealthy Ranger skills to sneak into her bed. She didn't know what that meant. They'd rarely fought when they were young, and nothing so serious as this. There was no precedent to give her any clue what to think or do.

Except, maybe there was. Their biggest fight before was about him going into the Army, and that hadn't even really been a fight so much as him making up his mind and telling her. He was a stubborn bastard when he wanted to be. If he'd truly convinced himself that he was no hero, that he wasn't worthy, that he'd failed, nothing she could say was going to change his mind. She hadn't been able to convince him not to leave her then. Why should now be any different?

A wave of fresh grief had tears burning in her eyes as she wondered how long it would take him to just come right out and say they were through?

When her phone rang, she lunged for it. But it wasn't Ty. Of course, it wasn't Ty. He'd left his phone last night when he'd stormed out. It was Caleb.

"Hey. Sorry to call so early, but I thought you'd want to hear this sooner rather than later. My brother, Mateo, is a former MMA fighter. He owns a gym now and has an apartment he keeps for helping domestic violence victims escape their abusers. It's open at the moment, and he says it's all yours, if you want it."

Paisley considered. Was she really going to leave? In the heat of the moment last night, she'd been determined to. Now... Could she really stay, knowing they were over and just waiting for the other shoe to drop? Having to endure that awful, painful emotional distance from him, knowing he was only still in her life because she was a case? She didn't even know if she'd have that. Ty had made it perfectly clear her situation was too much for him. She'd never intended to involve him in the first place. This would at least give her another option until she figured out what to do, and maybe it was a good idea to go to someone she had no connection to. She'd be harder to track that way.

"I'll take it."

"Great, I'll text you the information. When do you think you're coming?"

"As soon as I can get everything in my car." There were still things of hers at Ty's, but she'd get them sometime later. Right now, she needed distance from him.

She packed, quick and efficient. A part of her regretted the loss of a slow, relaxed morning that included breakfast from Athena Reynolds Maxwell, the award-winning chef sister who ran the kitchens of The Misfit Inn. But she needed to act. Too much of the past weeks had been spent in limbo, waiting for someone else to make a move. So, she hauled her things downstairs and out to her car, not even making a pass through the dining room for coffee. She'd pick some up on the road.

As she grabbed up the last of her stuff, she considered leaving a note of some kind for Ty. But what was she going to say? Leaving nothing, she shut the door. The room was in his name, so there wasn't even a need to properly check out.

"C'mon, Duke."

He trailed her downstairs and out the front door.

"You're leaving?"

The question came from Ari Bohannon. Pru's sixteen-year-old daughter was curled in one of the many chairs on the wrap-around porch. They'd bonded over romance Paisley's first night here. The girl reminded her so much of herself at that age. Full of cheerful, unwavering belief in love. And why shouldn't she be? She was surrounded on all sides by real-life examples in her parents and all of her aunts and their spouses. It was inspiring, really. Paisley had made a joke herself about what was in the water and inadvertently birthed a plot bunny about a hidden spring that made people fall in love. She and Ari had plotted half of it out the other day, which had proved a wonderful distraction. Paisley really hoped nothing destroyed the girl's romanticism. Contrary to Ty's opinion, the world needed more romantics.

"Yeah."

"Did Ty and Xander find the bad guy?"

"Um, no. Not as far as I know." And it said a lot about her headspace that she was less worried about the stalker and more worried about Ty at the moment.

"Are you going back home?"

Did the girl mean Nashville or Ty's? Did it matter? "I've imposed on y'all long enough." Which wasn't really an answer, she knew.

"You're not an imposition. You're a guest! That's what we're all about."

Her lips curved. "Spoken like a true innkeeper's daughter. But I do have to go. Someone's expecting me." Opening the door to the backseat, she shoved in Duke's dog bed and arranged it for the trip.

The girl was frowning when Paisley turned back around. "Are you and Ty okay?"

The question surprised her.

"I know it's none of my business, I just..." Ari pressed her lips together, as if to bite back the words. Paisley arched a brow and the girl burst out. "I wasn't trying to eavesdrop, but I heard y'all's fight last night, and then he left and hasn't come back, and this totally feels like the point for a dark period intervention."

Torn between a desire to laugh and cry, Paisley worked up a smile. "You're so much like I used to be, it's scary." She tossed her purse onto the front seat. "Sadly, real life doesn't adhere to scripted plot points. Doesn't mean that love's not worth it, but sometimes the timing is off. Or the other person might have a bigger wound than you know what to do with. Sometimes they need a wakeup call." *And sometimes love isn't enough.*

Ari frowned. "I'm going on record saying that this is a mistake."

"Noted." Paisley wasn't sure that it wasn't. But she didn't think there was a right move here. "It was cool to meet you Ari. I'll come back sometime, and we can hang. Maybe do some more plotting."

"I'd love that."

Paisley whistled. "C'mon, Duke. Time to go!"

But the dog didn't come immediately bounding over to the car at the magic word.

"Duke! Here boy."

Still, no jangle of tags or scrabble of paws.

"What has he gotten into? I swear to God, if he found something dead to roll in..."

She marched around the house, calling his name. Ari fell in with her. But by the time they'd circled the perimeter, there was no Duke. No barking. No sign of her beloved dog. Alarm overtook annoyance. "Where is he?"

"Don't worry. We'll find him," Ari assured her. "He probably just chased a bunny or something. I'll round up some more people to help look."

While she disappeared into the house, Paisley made another circuit in a wider circle, into the edge of the woods surrounding the property. Why couldn't it have rained or snowed recently so there were convenient paw prints leading her to her recalcitrant dog? More to the point, why had he wandered off? He hadn't pulled the escape artist routine since she'd first gotten him. Not since she'd stopped trying to put him in a crate. Maybe he was too overwhelmed by the fun and interesting stuff to sniff that they didn't have at home in the city.

A distant sound carried on the wind. Was that a bark?

"Duke!"

The sound came again. Definitely a bark.

Was he stuck somewhere? Taking off in the direction she thought she'd heard him, she shouted again, course correcting deeper into the woods. The bark was closer this time. Relief surged through her. He wasn't gone, and he didn't sound distressed. He'd just wandered too far and gotten into something.

Abruptly the sound cut off.

"Duke?"

Nothing.

There were cliffs around here. Caves. Hell, even bears. Her city-born dog was not prepared for any of that. Anxiety mounting again, Paisley ran faster, frantically scanning for a flash of tawny fur.

Something caught her shins, and she tumbled headlong into the dead leaves and dirt. Breathless from the impact, for a moment, she could only lie there, hands stinging. On a wheeze, she started to roll over and caught a flash of movement to the left.

She didn't even have time to draw breath for a scream before the figure in black was on her, wrenching her arms backward and pressing her into the ground. Adrenaline surged, and she tried to buck him off, but the knee in her back kept her pinned, her limbs flailing uselessly. Something sharp jabbed her in the hip. A needle? What the hell was he injecting her with?

Even as she could feel darkness creeping in, Paisley struggled to turn her head, to see her attacker. But all she could take in was a smear of clay across the toe of his dark brown hiking boots in the incongruous shape of a cross. Then there was nothing at all.

"GET UP."

A snapping voice cut through the questionable oblivion of sleep. As the sound tunneled through to Ty's brain, with it came awareness of pain. Instinctively, he fought to stay under, shrinking away from inevitable agony.

"Get up, damn it!"

"Honey, what are you—"

Something struck him. A solid but...soft? something. Not hard enough to really hurt but sufficient impact to drag him through another layer toward consciousness.

"If he's not up in the next thirty seconds, I'm hitting him with my stun gun instead of a pillow."

What the actual hell is going on?

Ty cracked his eyes open enough to catch a glimpse of an irate Ivy in the doorway before the slanting sunlight through the window forced him to slam them shut again. "I'm awake," he rasped.

"Harrison, go get him some pain killers. He doesn't deserve them, but he's going to need them."

For what? A dressing down? Like she could rival the drill sergeants he'd put up with in the Army? "What the hell has gotten into you?"

"Do you actually want to loll around and give Paisley a chance to decide to leave your ass, or do you want to fix this?"

Ty jack-knifed into an upright position and regretted it as the room spun on an unsteady axis. He gritted his teeth against the nausea. "What do you mean leave? She can't leave."

"She can and probably will if you don't do some serious damage control."

"Fuck." He vaulted out of bed, staggered and slapped a hand against the wall to steady himself. "Where's my phone?"

Harrison shrugged. "Must be in your truck up at the bar or back at the inn. Wasn't on you when we got back last night."

Ty couldn't get his brain to work as he tried to assess whether he was just hung over or still drunk. His head pounded like a helicopter blade was thrumming in his ears, and his eyes ached, but now that he was vertical, things were starting to stabilize. Not still drunk, then. This was what he got for drinking more than a beer for the first time in a year and a half and picking rot gut whiskey to do it.

"Shit. I didn't even text her where I was last night."

"I did. And I did you a solid by not mentioning you'd decided to take yourself on a bender."

"Thanks, man." He didn't need any further evidence of his weakness paraded in front of her. Willing himself steady, he took a few steps toward the door.

Ivy wrinkled her nose. "No matter what kind of apology you manage, Paisley isn't going to want to take you back if you smell like a distillery and look like something she scraped off her shoe. Get in the shower. I'll get you something of Harrison's to wear."

Ty squinted at her, desperately hoping the gesture didn't make his eyeballs pop out of their sockets. "You're going to help me?"

"Well, I didn't drag you awake *just* to yell at you."

"Thank you."

She pointed toward the bathroom. "Go!"

Because he needed more shock to his system,

he cranked the water to icy cold and stepped into the tub. Absorbing that fresh agony, he stood for a moment under the punishing spray, trying to logic his way through the situation and find the answers that had eluded him at the bottom of a bottle.

She'd had all night with his harsh words echoing in her head making her think...what? That he blamed her? That he was a weak, cowardly shadow of a man who couldn't protect her? That he wasn't even going to try anymore? That he didn't love her?

None of it was actually true, but he'd said or implied all of it. Of course, she'd want to leave. What the hell had he expected her to do? Just sit around being biddable until he pulled his head out of his ass enough to apologize? In all reality, he hadn't been thinking. He'd been reacting. And somewhere, deep down, a part of him had said it all to be proved right. That he wasn't worthy. That she'd ultimately get sick of his shit or disappointed enough to walk away.

Well, congratu-fucking-lations. Mission accomplished.

He had to get to her. He didn't know what he'd say when he did, but he'd cross that bridge when he got to it.

Fifteen minutes after his rude awakening, he

strode into the kitchen, feeling several steps below human. Harrison held out a tall glass with something resembling vomit inside.

"Do I wanna know what's in that?"

"I assure you, you do not. Here, take some aspirin with it."

Bracing himself, Ty tossed the pills back and gulped down the sludge. The indescribable horror of it made his eyes water. He slapped the empty glass down on the counter with a gasp. "Was there a raw egg in that?"

"I told you, you don't wanna know."

"Ty." At the sound of her voice, he turned to see Ivy standing in the doorway, face pale, green eyes scared.

The noxious brew he'd just downed turned to lead in his stomach. "What is it?"

"Ari just called. Duke is missing and now nobody can find Paisley. They were out looking, and Ari went to get more people to help. When she came back out, there was no sign of her. She's probably gone too deep in the woods and can't hear anyone call her."

Ty's heart thundered, dread and horror racing neck-and-neck through his system. "You don't really think that's what's going on."

"Do you?"

"No." The stalker knew about the dog. Had already demonstrated once that he could get close to him. What did Paisley love more than Duke? Nothing. She'd walk into hell itself to bring him back. And Ty had walked away, leaving her alone, foolishly believing she'd be safe among all the other guests and staff at the inn.

Harrison's hand settled on his shoulder. "Wherever your brain is going now, stop. You're no good to her if you spiral. Lock it down."

Drawing on all his training, he exhaled a long, slow breath, bullying the fear and the blame into a cell deep in his mind. There'd be time to deal with them later, when she was safe. As he felt the control click into place, he nodded. "Let's go'"

"I'll text Sebastian and be right behind you," Ivy promised.

Harrison drove. The whole way there, Ty prayed he was wrong. Prayed Paisley would be walking out of the woods with Duke at her side. But the people milling about in front of the three-story Victorian and the collection of extra vehicles parked all up and down the drive—including the sheriff—put that fragile hope to a swift death.

Spotting his boss at the center of a small crowd, Ty headed in his direction, Harrison on his heels. Xander looked grim as he held something out. "We found this."

Automatically, Ty accepted it, staring down at the bright turquoise case with the custom vinyl skin proclaiming *Please do not annoy the writer or she will put you in a book and kill you.* Paisley's cell phone. His jaw worked. "Where?"

"About half a mile due east. There—" Xander sighed, "there were signs of a struggle."

The beast Ty had locked away roared and rattled the bars on its cage. He closed his eyes and allowed himself a single moment to acknowledge the rage. At himself. At whoever had taken his woman. "What do we know?"

"She was planning to leave." This came from Ari, who'd been Paisley's shadow since she arrived at the inn.

Ty focused in on her, noting the mix of fear and teenage belligerence in her dark eyes. "She what?'"

"She'd packed her car and everything to go back to Nashville because you were an idiot."

"Ari!" Pru's reprimand was horrified and sharp.

"Not helping," Xander added.

Ty absorbed the words and the guilt they inspired. He'd driven her away even before she'd been taken. Ivy had surmised as much, but the confirmation still rocked him. "She's not wrong." Pushing past self-recrimination, he turned to the girl. "Did she tell anyone she was going?"

"She said someone was expecting her, but she didn't say who."

It had been less than twenty-four hours. He felt in his gut she hadn't made this call before last night, which meant the stalker had been close, waiting. How close? "Are all the guests accounted for?"

Pru's eyes went wide. "Are you suggesting one of them could have taken her?"

"Process of elimination," Xander explained.

Pru's husband, Flynn, was already headed toward the house. "I'll go check."

"Did you see anyone else out this morning? Did anyone?" Ty glanced around at the others gathered, including them in the question.

"It's midweek so we don't have a full house," Kennedy explained. "Three guests have been up and at breakfast in the dining room, and we haven't opened for the day's spa appointments."

Xander studied him. "What are you thinking?"

"That Duke is the friendliest dog in the world, and it doesn't take much to lure him off. I think he was used as bait."

"Are there security cameras?" Harrison asked.

"No," Xander started. "We never—"

But Ty was already running for the house. He bolted up the front porch and through the door. He took the stairs two at a time, racing for their third-floor room.

His duffel bag was still where he'd left it, his work boots kicked over by the chair. But all traces of Paisley and Duke were gone. Her absence struck him like a fist, but he couldn't take the time to absorb it. He lunged for his laptop, even as footsteps sounded on the stairs.

"What the hell?" Xander asked from the doorway.

"I installed cameras when we moved in."

"Are you serious?" Ty couldn't quite tell if there was censure beneath the shock in his boss's voice.

"I'm a paranoid bastard. They aren't permanent."

He pulled up the system, scrolling back the video feeds to about forty-five minutes before as both Xander and Harrison peered over his shoulders.

"Where the hell are these?" Xander asked. "I didn't see a thing outside."

"Hidden in the eaves of the house. They're small."

"We used all kinds of fun surveillance equipment in the Army," Harrison added.

"There."

Duke came into the frame, tail high as he performed his familiar sniffing examination of the side yard. Abruptly his head shot up, ears pricking, and his tail began to wag. He bolted out of view. Toggling over to a different view, Ty could just make out a figure, head down, beckoning the dog from the edge of the woods. He crouched down, giving the dog an easy rubdown, clearly offering him treats that Duke gobbled down without even chewing.

"C'mon, you fucker. Stand up and show your face," Ty muttered.

As if following orders, the guy snapped a leash on Duke and rose, taking one last look toward the front of the house and giving Ty a clear view of his face.

"Oh, fuck no."

14

Muted but frantic barking jerked Paisley to consciousness.

Duke.

She turned her head toward the sound, straining to see. But there was only blackness, and the motion made her muscles scream. Everything hurt and her mind seemed shrouded in fog. She tried to swallow, only to find something blocking her tongue. The strangeness of that dragged her back to awareness.

Not something. A gag. And she couldn't see because she was blindfolded. Her arms and feet were immobilized. Bound to a chair? Wood creaked as she strained to move. The rest of it came back in a rush. The woods. She was attacked. Drugged.

Fresh fear spiked beneath the remnants of the drugs. Where was she? How long had she been out? Where was her kidnapper? She couldn't hear anything over the roaring of her pulse and Duke's continued barking. He was alive, and he was nearby. That was...something. Struggling to calm herself, she inventoried her body. Aches from the fall, soreness from where her arms had been wrenched back. But she didn't feel any major injuries or signs of violation.

For the moment, she seemed to be alone. No doubt, that wouldn't last. What was her kidnapper's end game? This whole thing had begun as such comparatively benign contact to have escalated this far. What the hell did he want? Was he planning to keep her, *Misery* style? Was she expected to be some kind of plaything?

Closing her eyes, she wished desperately for Ty. Did he even know she was gone? If he knew, he was looking for her. No matter what headspace he was in, so long as she was in danger, he wouldn't stop trying to find her. She knew that beyond the shadow of a doubt. He was going to come for her. She just had to hold on until he did.

The shriek of rusty hinges echoed through the space. A space that sounded far larger than she'd imagined. Paisley repressed a scream as footsteps made their way across a creaky wooden floor, wondering if she should pretend to still be unconscious. But she couldn't stop from jerking her head toward the sound, trying to track the movement as the person circled around her. Clearing the room? Rescue? Ty?

A low, male voice cursed and rushed toward her. At the sense of hands near her face, Paisley flinched. The blindfold slid away.

"It's okay. I've gotcha."

She blinked unfocused eyes at the man kneeling in front of her chair. Not Ty. Joel Fisher.

He holstered his service weapon and moved behind her to work the gag free. As soon as it was out of her mouth, she flexed her jaw, trying to get feeling back.

"Are you okay?"

She was too stupefied to see him to focus on anything else. "I...what are you...how are you here?"

With a wry half smile, he began to work at the knots on her ankles. "Just call me the cavalry. I was already on my way up here, so I joined in the search when you disappeared."

"How long have I been missing?"

"Since this morning."

So it had been hours, not potential days.

"Why were you even coming here?" Where was here? Was she still somewhere in Eden's Ridge?

"Deputy Brooks called to discuss the transfer of your protective detail. I understand you've had some problems up here. We've got a safehouse ready back in Nashville." Joel paused, his hands on her knees, and looked up with an expression she couldn't quite read. Earnestness mixed with...a sort of manic adoration. "I'm going to keep you safe."

Something about this didn't feel right. Ty didn't like Joel and wasn't particularly impressed with him as a detective. Maybe that was colored by jealousy, but even if he was abdicating his own role in her case, he'd find someone he knew and trusted to pass it to.

"Let me get your hands loose." He straightened, and her gaze dropped to his feet and the dark brown boots he wore. Mud was splattered across the toe of one. Paisley angled her head, squinting at the shape it made. A cross.

Oh my God.

Panicked adrenaline dumped into her system, but she said nothing as Joel began to untie her wrists. She needed her hands free if she was going to do anything. And what the hell was she going to actually do? Wiggling her feet, trying to get the feeling back into her toes and legs, she finally took a look at her surroundings, searching for anything she might use as a weapon.

She was in a church. Or what had once been one. Much of the glass in the lancet windows was cracked or gone entirely. What remained was obscured by a layer of filth. A handful of old wooden pews marched in uneven rows toward where she sat. The pulpit—or where one must have sat—was behind her. A large, broken cross leaned against the raised platform of the dais. There was nothing she could swing. Nothing she could even move in her current condition except the chair she sat in. If there was a door other than the one he'd come through, she couldn't see it from her position.

The pressure on her arms released at last. On a relieved sigh, Paisley hunched forward, rubbing at her wrists and hands. She needed to buy some time. Every extra minute was another one for the drugs to wear off. And another one that actual help might be on the way.

"Duke. Is Duke okay?"

"He's fine, I think. Sounds it, anyway. I spotted him in a crate out back."

What kind of crate will actually hold my little Houdini? She could hear it now, the sound of him rattling the cage. "Why hasn't anybody let him loose yet?"

"I was more concerned with you." He held out his hands to draw her to her feet.

"I can do it. I need to do it." Stubbornly, she shoved to her feet, swaying a little. "You're here alone?"

"Yes. We split up to search for you. I followed a wild hunch and ended up here. We need to hurry. We don't know when this guy will come back."

Moving behind the chair so she could use the back for balance, she insisted, "I'm not going anywhere." If she changed locations, how much harder would it be for Ty and his people to find her?

Confusion flickered over his face. "What? Of course, you are. You can't stay here."

Paisley shook her head, brain frantically trying to find a way out of this. How could she keep stalling him? "I'm not going to live running forever, always looking over my shoulder. I can be bait. You can call for backup. He has to come back for me eventually, and y'all can take him down."

A muscle ticked in Joel's jaw. "That's not an option. We need to go."

"Why isn't it an option, Joel?"

Again with the jaw clenching. He definitely hadn't counted on her being noncompliant.

"There's no radio signal here. We have to hike out to get one."

"On the radio you're not carrying? Or is it because you're not going to call for backup? Because you don't want to be caught?"

"What are you talking about? Did he hit you over the head?"

"I recognize your shoes from when you took me down."

He closed his eyes and sighed. "Why couldn't you just do what you were supposed to?"

Seeing her opening, she shoved the chair into him with all her might, hoping to knock him off balance. Seconds. It was only going to buy her seconds. But she lunged for the door, dodging pews and broken floorboards. Her hand curled around the knob, yanking it open. She hurtled outside, into weak, winter sunlight. For one glorious moment, she thought she'd make it. But Joel snagged her around the waist.

"Let me go!"

He yanked her off her feet, pivoting them both back inside.

But not before she saw the streak of her dog loose and racing into the woods.

As it was the last place Paisley was seen, the Misfit Inn had been turned into incident command. Search and rescue had been deployed, combing the woods more thoroughly, searching for any additional clues. Ty had called Metro Police in Nashville to confirm what he already knew—that Fisher wasn't around. He'd taken personal leave four days before. That wasn't an indictment on its own, but the report from Carissa Knowles, who'd co-taught the citizen's police academy with him was a heavy weight on that side of the scale.

"He really liked her. Everybody did. She was the belle of the class, and everybody had more fun because she was there. But Fisher definitely skated the line with her. Flirting even though she was taken. Touching her more than strictly necessary. She definitely got special treatment and special attention. He got a charge out of all her questions. Like they made him feel all important—big man on campus, as it were. Which was especially affecting for him because he went through a nasty divorce a couple years before. He didn't take it well when he asked her out and she shot him down."

"What did he do?"

"To her face, nothing. But there was plenty of

that grown-man sulking. He stayed some kind of friends with her. In my opinion, he thought he could wait her out until she was single again. But that didn't work out for him either. She never went out with him so far as I know."

That tracked with what Paisley had told him herself. "Are you aware of any history of sexual harassment or other inappropriate behavior from Fisher toward anyone else?"

"He's had a few slaps on the wrist, but no formal sexual harassment charges. And that's entirely because many of our superiors are cut from the same cloth."

"Do you know anything about her case?"

"I knew she'd been up here for something, but not specifically what. Let me see what's in the system." The clack of keys sounded in the background. "There is no case."

"What?"

"There's not a damned thing in the system after the mugging. If he was investigating this, he was doing it off-book."

What better way to hide his own involvement than to control the flow of information to authorities? "Thank you for your help."

"If there's anything else I can do, don't hesitate to let me know."

Hanging up, Ty relayed the conversation to Ivy.

"So, he meets her at the citizens police academy, falls for her charm, develops an attachment, and gets shot down. The next month she's mugged, and who does she turn to? Fisher. But she still doesn't take the hint. Doesn't take it past the professional into the personal he wants. Then the packages start. Nothing major. Just enough to creep her out. Again, she turns to her buddy. She's getting more and more agitated and worried as things progress. But then you come into the picture, and she turns to you instead of him. That's when we see the big jump and escalation. Because she's going off his script. Everything that he's done since then has been to get her away from you."

Ty's hands curled to fists. "Yeah, well, it worked."

Ivy waved that off, frowning as she continued to work the problem in her head. "But why take her now? If he wants to be the good guy, the one she turns to, how does this support that goal?"

"Why does that matter? He took her. End of story."

"Because it tells us something about how much direct danger she's in. Whether this is somehow a continuation of some elaborate hoax or if he's fallen into the territory of 'If I can't have her, no one can.' For the record, all the evidence points to the former."

"It's all a good theory, but we need evidence. Leads. Where the hell did he take her? The BOLO on his vehicle hasn't turned up anything. We don't know if he's on his way back to Nashville or if he's gone to ground here."

"Metro PD is sending someone to his house," Xander reported.

"We need copies of his financials and phone records," Leanne added. "I'm working on getting a warrant for that."

"So far, the property search isn't turning up much. Other than his house in Nashville, nothing's coming up," Laurel reported. "If he's got some-where specific to take her, it's either not his or the deed is in someone else's name. You said he was divorced. Maybe there's something under the ex-wife."

Ty paced a restless circuit around the room. "This is all taking too much time." He'd had her for nearly four hours. That was long enough to get back to Nashville or even leave the state entirely.

"It's what we've got," Xander said easily. "Everybody in town is keeping a lookout for Paisley and Duke. The phone tree and the town's social media were updated. We're doing the best we can."

Before he could roar that it wasn't good enough, Paisley's cell phone began to ring. The number flashing on the screen wasn't in her contacts and had a local prefix.

Ty snatched it up. "Hello?"

"Yes, uh, are you missin' a dog?"

His hands tightened on the phone. "Yes. Who is this?"

"Mel Jackson. This friendly fella came running out of the woods by my house. Ran right on up to me. I saw he had a collar and corralled him so he couldn't run off again."

"Can you describe the dog?"

"Looks like some kind of shepherd lab mix. Mostly kind of tan with some white on his chest, black on his tail. This number was on his collar."

An iota of relief trickled through. "That's Duke. Is he injured?"

"Seems fine to me. Pretty agitated though."

"I'm coming to get him. Where are you?" He took down the address and hung up. "Duke just showed up at Mel Jackson's place out on Sweet Gum Road."

Xander frowned. "That's all the way on the other side of the county."

"What's near there?"

"Not much. Some farmland. Forest. The old Eary settlement."

"What's that?"

"It was a town back in the eighteen hundreds. Porter could tell you more about why it was abandoned than I could. He was always more into history than I was. But anyway, what passes for roads have been overgrown for decades. I haven't been out there in years, but last time I was there, very little was still standing. Mostly a bunch of structures that collapsed years ago."

"There's a church." Everybody turned to Laurel, who flipped her laptop around. "It's on a couple of sites for abandoned places."

"You think he could've taken her there?" Leanne asked.

"I don't know. Duke wouldn't have made it that far on foot. But as you've pointed out, it'd be hard to get in and out of with an unconscious or unwilling person. It's just as possible Fisher dumped the dog over that way in hopes of distracting us while he gets the hell out of Dodge." But Ty's gut was screaming that this was the break they needed. He exchanged a look with Harrison and Sebastian. "I'm going to get him."

Harrison pushed up. "I'll drive you to pick him up."

"I'll follow you out and look him over, just to make sure he's really fine," Sebastian added.

Xander jerked his head toward the inn office. "All three of you."

Despite the fact that he was itching to leave, Ty followed his boss inside.

Xander kept his voice low. "I wasn't born yesterday. What the hell are you planning?"

"I'm going to get Paisley's dog."

"You think she's up at Eary."

"Maybe," Ty allowed.

"I can talk to Chris about pulling the SAR team back. But it'll take time to reconvene over there."

Ty shook his head. "It'll take time and might be a waste of it. There's no need to pull them off the search where they are without more evidence. I want to check it out. I might just be chasing my own tail, but if he does have her up there, a small, highly trained team is much more likely to be able to get to her without being detected. SAR teams are trained to make noise so the lost will hear them. We're trained to be ghosts."

Dark eyes studied his. "I don't like it. But I'm aware you're gonna do it anyway, so you're damned well gonna stop by the station first. These two need tactical gear."

"Thank you."

"Don't do anything I'm gonna have to arrest you for."

Ty's mouth twitched. "Understood."

With the stop by the Sheriff's Department to pick up gear and Ty's cruiser, it took longer than he wanted to get to Mel Jackson's place. As soon as he pulled up, the front door opened, and a grizzled old guy in an ancient Army jacket edged out. Ty recognized him as one of the veterans who volunteered as security up at the courthouse.

"Mr. Jackson? I'm Deputy Brooks. We spoke about the dog."

"He belongs to your little lady." Mel's sober tone made it clear he'd finally heard the news about Paisley's disappearance.

"Yes."

Nodding once, Mel opened the door again and Duke bulleted out, making straight for Ty, barking with none of his usual joy. The sound was deeper, more forceful. He stopped just out of arm's reach and stamped his feet before wheeling and running a little ways back toward the woods. He stopped, offering another sharp bark and stomp.

Sebastian shut his truck door. "Is he doing what I think he's doing?"

Sending up a prayer to whatever deity might be listening, Ty popped his trunk. "If there's a God, he's pulling a Lassie. Suit up."

<h1 style="text-align:center">15</h1>

Paisley was strapped back to the damned chair, this time with plastic cuffs. If she'd been able to move her arms, she could've broken free. Joel had taught her how to do that himself during the citizen's police academy. But without some slack to build up momentum, she was stuck. She'd expected him to drug her again and haul her off to wherever he'd been planning. He hadn't even tried. She realized he hadn't come prepared for that. Wherever they were was remote, and he didn't seem to have a vehicle nearby to just drive them out. He'd well and truly expected her to hike out with him like a good little rescued kidnapping victim.

Well, she'd screwed that, hadn't she?

But as Joel continued to restlessly pace the church, tunneling his fingers through his hair and muttering, she wasn't sure that was a good thing. He didn't really want to hurt her. For all he'd manhandled her, he'd used only as much force as necessary to subdue her. If she had waited to make her move until they were somewhere less remote, when other people were around, or even until they were further into the woods where she might've found a handy branch or something, maybe she could have managed a true escape.

Too late now.

She hadn't played into his narrative and now there was no going back.

His agitation made it clear he wasn't great at thinking on his feet. He wanted to consider all the angles. How long until he figured out there was no getting out of this situation? He'd kidnapped her. Presumably, he was the one behind the harassment that had stolen her peace of mind. There wasn't a chance in hell she'd let him just get away with that, which meant he couldn't afford to let her walk away.

Paisley didn't like any of the outcomes of that scenario.

Maybe if she got him talking about something else so he couldn't actively consider what to do, it would buy more time. Duke was free. If Joel had noticed, he hadn't let on, and she wasn't going to point it out. Surely her incredibly social dog would find the nearest person, who'd notify someone. People would be looking for her by now. She just needed to give them a chance to get to her.

"This isn't how things were supposed to turn out," he muttered. "Not at all."

"How were they supposed to turn out? How was all this supposed to work?" She let genuine curiosity rather than scorn fill her voice. The writer in her really wanted to know, and focusing on that helped keep the panic at bay.

His head shot up, his eyes full of frustrated misery. "We were supposed to get out of here. Successful rescue and proof that I can keep you safe. Then we'd head back to the safehouse in Nashville, so you'd finally spend the time you need with me to get to know me and see. You just needed time."

"See what?"

"That we're meant to be. I knew it almost from the first time I met you. You're the first person who made me feel like somebody after the divorce. You treated me like I had value. Like I wasn't a middle-aged loser, who'd peaked too soon, going nowhere in a cheap suit. Like I had something to offer. We were friends, you and I. And it was so clear we have the potential to be more." He gently skimmed his fingers over her cheek, his expression soft.

Paisley fought not to flinch away from the touch.

"I needed that. I needed you. I got that you weren't single when I asked you out after the academy. But once you were, you kept saying no."

As the softness melted back into frustration, she swallowed. "I wasn't in a place for a relationship. I told you that."

"I know. So, I wanted to position myself to be there for you when you were."

"I don't understand." *Keep him talking. Play dumb. Get a confession.*

"I just wanted to scare you a little," he admitted. "It was way too easy to do. You really need to be more aware of your surroundings when you're out in public."

"*You?* The mugging was you?" She'd assumed he'd sent the packages, but she didn't have to feign shock at this. She'd trusted him. Believed he had her best interests at heart.

The more fool me.

"You were supposed to turn to me. I'm the one who was there for you. I'm the one who cared. But it was business as usual after that. So, I had to get creative. Find something to nudge you back into my orbit."

"So, you...what? Made up a fake crazy fan?"

"It was child's play, really, after the stuff you talked about at the academy. You have such a vivid imagination. It seemed like a low-threat option that would be easy to do away with once I didn't need it anymore. It was never supposed to go this far. But you didn't do what you were supposed to. You turned to *him*."

Reminding him of Ty didn't seem like a good idea.

"Why? I don't understand why you'd go to such lengths—creating some kind of false danger—just to get my attention."

Joel stared at her as if that were the most obvious piece of this whole mess. "I wanted to be your hero."

"You have a gross misunderstanding about what a hero is." The words were out before she could think better of them.

His bitter snort echoed off the rafters. "I suppose you'll say a hero is supposed to be like Ty Brooks. Small town deputy and your old *friend*."

Paisley didn't quite manage to stop the roll of her eyes at his derision. He had no idea who Ty really was. The motion put one of the windows in her periphery. Was that movement or just the trees shifting in the wind?

"Tell me, Paisley, what is it he has that I don't? Why did you choose him?"

Ignoring the question, she opted to educate. For now, he was listening to her. If she could keep him engaged, it would buy more time, and this was a topic she could talk about for hours. "Heroism is not about physical protection from danger. It's not about feats of derring-do. Those are men's definitions—and yeah, they're valid, but they aren't the only kinds of heroism out there. For most women, they aren't even the most important. I mean, I like a badass as much as the next gal, but most of us don't live lives where that's relevant all the time."

Warming to her topic, she tried to lean forward, only to be stopped by the cuffs. "For me, heroism is about being what I need. Seeing what needs doing and doing it because you can. Making my life easier in a million tiny ways, like picking up my favorite wine on the way home because you know I had a lousy writing day or walking the dog and making breakfast in bed because I was up too late. Doing the vacuuming because you remember that one time I ran over my toe right after I had surgery and have a little bit of trauma about it. You talk about wanting me to see you. That's exactly what this is about. Seeing your partner for who they really are as a person. Not as a glorified ideal. Not as a maid or a mother or a plaything. That's the number one complaint I hear from my readers. That their partners don't *see* them. That goes beyond annoyances like leaving the toilet seat up or dirty clothes all over the floor. Women want men who will wade into the trenches of everyday life, not just making sure the doors are locked at night and sleeping on the side of the bed closest to the door in case the boogieman breaks in or whatever other things the patriarchy has deemed acceptable masculine behaviors. They want actual partners."

Joel was staring at her like she'd grown a second head. That was fine. She wasn't really talking to him anymore.

"That's not heroic," he insisted.

"To the exhausted mom of two, who hasn't slept in weeks, or the career woman trying to get a promotion and juggle her marriage it is. Really, it's not your fault for not understanding that. You're a victim of toxic masculinity. Decades of programming designed to maintain the status quo. And where's that gotten you? Divorced from a marriage where probably neither of you really saw each other, married to a job I'm not entirely sure you actually like, well down the path of what started out as an effort to think outside the box and has devolved into a problematic hot mess in the middle of freaking nowhere, with the woman you purport to care about tied to a chair."

He had the grace to wince at that.

"You wanted to know what Ty has that you don't, why I chose him? History. A long and involved one that finally brought us back together after years apart. I love him. I've always loved him, flaws and all. And it has nothing to do with the fact that he's a former Army Ranger who currently has a gun trained on your head."

The door burst open.

Paisley threw her weight to the side, tipping the chair as Joel reached for his gun and spun. Shots rang out, and she screamed, watching Joel's body buck and fall into one of the pews, knocking it askew. Footsteps thundered inside, accompanied by a tawny blur. Snarling and snapping, her precious, peaceable dog sank his teeth into Joel's ass. The weak, wheezing howl proved her kidnapper was not, in fact, dead.

Moving, swift and efficient, Ty closed the distance, kicking Joel's gun out of reach. Beyond him, Harrison and Sebastian moved in, their own weapons trained on the writhing man. None of them did anything to deter Duke.

"Aren't you going to stop him?" Paisley demanded.

Lowering his weapon, Ty set it aside and righted her chair. "I mean, at least one of us deserves to get a piece of him. Duke's the one who led us to you, so by rights, he gets dibs."

"You already shot him!"

"Bean bag round. Doesn't count. Though he's probably got a few cracked or busted ribs by the sound of that breathing." Crouching down, he cupped her cheek. "You okay?"

"Shaken up. Little sore. But yeah. He didn't hurt me."

Ty's throat worked, and his lips finally twitched into something resembling a smile. "Only you would manage to distract a kidnapper with a lecture on the patriarchy and toxic masculinity."

She searched his face, soaking in the sight of him and wondering how much he'd heard. "It wasn't just for his benefit."

Dropping his gaze, he pulled out a tactical knife and began slicing through the plastic cuffs.

Understanding now wasn't the time, she took

pity on the still screaming Joel. "Duke! Come here, baby."

With one last bark, as if to say, "And don't you forget it!" her dog trotted over, tail wagging, mouth spread in a broad, canine grin. He rubbed against her, whining, licking. As soon as her hands were free, she wrapped her arms around him. "You're such a good boy. As soon as we get home, I'm getting you the biggest, juiciest steak I can find."

She felt Ty pull back even before he walked over to Joel, yanking his hands behind his back and slapping on cuffs. "You're under arrest for kidnapping, assault, breaking and entering, and that's just for starters."

Joel screamed again as Ty hauled him to his feet. "I need...medical attention."

"Yeah, you'll get it. Eventually. That's the thing, though. You picked such an out-of-the-way place, it's gonna take us a while to get you back for any. So you're gonna have to deal with that well-deserved mess Duke made of your butt cheek. Meanwhile, you've got the right to remain silent."

He finished mirandizing Joel and only then radioed back to report she'd been found and make arrangements for extraction. By the time more help had arrived, he still hadn't touched her again. He'd hardly even looked at her. As she slid onto the back of an ATV—with Harrison instead of Ty —Paisley accepted that the mission was over, objective achieved, and she was going to have to find a way to live with letting him go.

NIGHT HAD FALLEN by the time all the formalities were taken care of. Fisher's wounds had been treated, and he was in a cell. Despite the offer to put it off, Paisley had insisted on giving her statement. Ty had listened to her account of events, thinking of what might have happened and feeling sick. Then he'd offered his own statement, grateful there'd been nothing he needed to edit out. He'd gone prepared for deadly force, but he wasn't sorry he hadn't needed to use it. Paisley had enough trauma to sort through without adding that to the list, and by-the-book meant there was less chance Fisher would weasel out of this on any kind of technicality. There'd be paperwork—there was always paperwork—but that could wait.

Xander laid down his pen, flexing his hand. "I'm sure we'll have more questions. But for now, you're both free to go."

Paisley shoved back from the table. "My car is back at the inn."

Ty grabbed his keys. "I'll drive you."

They loaded up in the cruiser, Duke in the back, Paisley in the front passenger seat. Silence lay heavy between them as Ty pulled out of the lot. He didn't miss the arms she crossed over her middle or the way she didn't look at him.

No more putting off the inevitable.

"I need to say some things."

He felt rather than saw her tense.

"Okay."

"I'm sorry. The list of what for is getting pretty long, at this point. I was all kinds of out of line last night. I got too much in my head, listened too much to my demons. I should never have said those things, and I sure as hell shouldn't have left you alone and vulnerable. I swore I'd protect you, and instead I was a complete ass and made you feel like it was better to leave than stay and deal with me."

She glanced over in surprise. "You knew I was leaving?"

"Ari kinda read me the riot act about it."

Paisley huffed a little laugh. "Me, too." She turned her focus back to the passing dark. "Last night feels like a lifetime ago. I appreciate your apology, Ty, but it seems like we're even on all of that. You did what you set out to do. You caught the person behind all this." Her tone was off. Strained somehow.

"You sound...not entirely happy about that."

Her shoulders twitched. "It was someone I considered a friend, so that's got me questioning my judgement."

"You said something about that before. About how you hadn't ever dated anyone you didn't think was a good person. You never went out with him."

"Because I didn't think we were a good fit, and I wasn't attracted. Not because deep down I recognized he was stalker material. I looked at him with rose-colored glasses, and look where it got me."

"I've always liked the fact that you see the best in people."

"I don't know if I'll be able to keep doing that. I think it will take some time for me to accept it's over. That I'm safe and don't have to keep looking over my shoulder. But it's more that I'm sad that we're over."

The words slid between Ty's ribs like a blade, sparking panic. Had everything she'd said in the church been a lie? Just something intended to distract Fisher, so they had a chance to move in? He tightened his hands on the wheel as she kept talking.

"I mean... it's not that I didn't expect this in the

beginning. You were very clear about what you had to offer. It was just the threat to me that changed the rules. Now that's past, and you're realizing that nothing really changed for you. I get it. I hate it, but I get it. I was the foolish one who went and fell in love with you again. That's on me. I don't blame you for not feeling the same."

Unable to listen to any more of this, Ty whipped the car to the shoulder and turned to her. "What the actual fuck are you talking about? *Everything* changed, even when I didn't want it to. I admit I kinda lost my shit with the case, and I said some unconscionable things in the process, but I haven't changed my mind about wanting you. I was working out how to best grovel for a second chance when I found out you were missing. I didn't get that far, what with the search, so let me just be blunt. I love you. I've always loved you. And even though I fucked up, even though I hurt you, and I have no right to ask for anything, I'm begging you not to give up on us. Not to give up on me."

Paisley launched herself across the car. Or tried. The seatbelt and console and computer stopped her. "Oh, for the love of—of all the times to not be in your truck with a bench seat." She unsnapped her seatbelt and stretched far enough to frame his face in both her hands. "I don't want to give up on us, and I'll never give up on you."

He tried to close the distance between them, only to be stopped by his own seatbelt. Swearing, he yanked it off and reached for her, not caring that he bumped his elbows on all the suddenly inconvenient, pain-in-the-ass equipment. He needed to get his hands, his mouth on her.

At the first taste of her lips, Ty nearly drowned in the flood of relief. She wasn't leaving. She wasn't giving up on him. He hadn't lost her to his own fear and stupidity. Burying his hands in her hair, he struggled to get closer. Her mouth open under his, as desperate and greedy as he was to wipe out all the hurt and distance of the last days. He wanted skin, wanted to claim her in every way he knew how. Her fingers scrabbled at his shirt, not managing more than a few buttons before the damned console got in the way. Abandoning the shirt, she reached across to his lap, palming his straining erection.

"Need you," she murmured on a frustrated moan he felt down to his marrow.

"Likewise." Starving for the taste of her, he captured her mouth again.

He was on the verge of considering something drastic and skating the line of public indecency when someone honked. Ty jerked back in time to see headlights passing them by outside the steamed-up windows. "This is really not the place for this." Clearing his throat, he forced himself to release her and settled back into his seat. "Buckle up." As she did, he hit defrost and put the car back into gear with shaking hands.

"Turn around."

"What?"

Paisley curled a hand around his arm. "My stuff will keep. Take me home, Galahad. I want to make love with you in our bed."

He hadn't let himself dream for years, but here she was, handing him the one he'd harbored in the deepest chamber of his heart. He'd make sure she didn't regret it.

"Yes ma'am."

16

Paisley knew she should be sleeping. Mentally and emotionally exhausted after the events of the day, tucked safely in Ty's arms, she should've been completely unconscious. But her brain was going ninety miles an hour, careening from one thing to another like a pinball.

Ty loved her. He loved her. He loved her. It echoed through her head like the most glorious refrain. He wasn't letting her go. He wasn't ending things. She didn't want to do long distance. He wouldn't do as well in the city, and he'd need the continued support of Harrison and Sebastian. She could work anywhere. She wanted to decide all the things, right now, to lock this down so that the warmth of his skin against hers and the feel of his heartbeat beneath her palm was her every night and the mission of making him smile was her every day. No more waiting. No more angsting. But it was too soon for all that. Hours after a kidnapping was not the time to make major life decisions.

"You're thinking so loud, it's echoing off the ceiling." His voice was rusty with sleep.

"Sorry," she whispered, pressing a kiss to his chest.

He resumed the lazy circles on her back, a gesture somewhere between soothing and arousing that had sent him into sleep after a stupendous and athletic round of makeup sex. She mirrored the motion on his chest. Neither of them could get enough touching. "What's on your mind?"

Paisley snuggled in closer against him, twining her leg with his. "I want to sell my house." The hand stroking her back stopped. "I was thinking about it already before today. Yesterday? Whatever. I don't think I'll be able to go back to living there after everything that happened."

"You could always turn it into an AirBnB for a while, to give yourself time to be sure."

"I mean, maybe, because that would actually be a good investment. But I am sure. You're here, so that's where I want to be." When he didn't immediately respond, her heart leapt into a frantic tattoo. "Not that I'm forcing my way into just moving in with you without asking. I'm not trying to rush things."

His bark of laughter interrupted the panic. "I don't think anybody can accuse us of rushing things. Twenty years is quite long enough." With a heave, he rolled to face her, tucking her hair back behind one ear. "If you *want* your own place, that's fine. I pushed you into moving in with me without actually asking what you want, and you've had a lot of stress and changes. I completely understand if you'd rather have some room to breathe. But if that's just out of some sense that I need space from you, forget it. I've had space. I don't want any more."

The growing erection pressing against her belly underscored the point. Paisley wriggled against him with a smirk. "I can tell."

"Minx." He gently nipped her mouth, wrapping his arms around her. "I want to find *our* place. We'll need a bigger one, with a proper fenced yard for Duke, a bedroom with an actual door, a deck for entertaining—"

Paisley tipped back so she could look at him, sure he was being facetious. "You want to entertain?"

"With you? Yes. Everything's more fun with

you. Anyway, there should be a master bath, with a big ass soaker tub for two and a walk-in shower."

Getting into the spirit of things, she began to grin. "With multiple jets."

"Naturally. A kitchen with actual counter space for all the cooking we're going to do together."

"We're going to cook together?"

"All the time. Especially weekend breakfasts that are going to end up with us back in bed."

"I'm definitely liking the sound of this."

"Me, too. You'll need an office space, of course."

"And there should be a library."

"We should definitely have a library," he agreed. "One with big, cushy furniture and maybe a fireplace."

The idea of it charmed and excited her and made her remember the drawers of books under the couch. "I found yours."

His brows drew together. "My what?"

"Your library drawers under the couch."

"Ah. I had to get creative with storage. There aren't many empty walls for shelves in this place."

Would he tell her about his favorite if she asked? It seemed a less sensitive question now. "I saw my books in there."

"I told you I'd read them."

She hadn't quite believed him and had been too caught up in mortification at what those books had revealed about her in their years apart. "Yeah. Some looked like more than once."

"Sure."

"Why *Edge of Reason*? It looked pretty well loved, like there was something you kept coming back to, over and over."

"There was. Remember how I mentioned you write like you talk?"

"Yeah."

"There was that passage after the bombing, when Boone and Layla are trapped and think they aren't going to survive." His eyes unfocused a little. "He said, 'Home isn't a place for people like us. It's not white picket fences or comfortable beds or hallways lined with photographs chronicling the years and the milestones. Home is a feeling. It's the scent of your hair. The feel of your hand in mine. The flash of your smile. The sound of your laugh or the way you slurp noodles so fast they slap your nose. It's a thousand tiny moments that all add up to one truth: Home is you. It always was.'"

He blinked, focusing back on her. "When I read it, I could hear you in my head, and it was like you were talking directly to me. When things got hard, I'd pull it out to remind me. Because you were always home to me."

Paisley's throat went thick with tears. "Ty."

Stroking back her hair, he searched her face in the dim glow of the night light that illuminated the stairs. "Thank you for letting me come home."

She pressed her brow to his. "It was always yours. I've just been waiting for you to come back to me."

For a long time, they lay there in the dark, breathing the same air, content to finally be where they were meant to. Together. Lulled by the steady rhythm of his breath, Paisley was on the edge of sleep when he spoke again.

"Can I ask you something?"

"Anything."

After a beat of weighted silence, he sucked in a breath. "Will you help me go home for real? Come with me to the celebration of Garrett's life?"

She understood what it would cost him to go. Understood, too, what it meant that he wanted her with him. It was the next step in his journey to healing, and she was going to be right there by his side. "I wouldn't miss it."

~

TY SLID OUT of his truck and into the golden spring day. Being in March, Garrett's birthday had always been hit or miss on weather, as likely to be incessant rain and wind as sun. But Bethany had lucked out with her planning, getting a gorgeous, warm day that called for shirt sleeves and iced tea. As he looked the rest of the way up the drive toward the neat farmhouse where she'd grown up, Ty remembered others just like it, walking shoulder-to-shoulder with his best friend, tossing a football and laughing while they decided what trouble to get into for the afternoon.

Welcome home, brother.

The phantom sound of Garrett's voice had a chill racing over Ty's skin, despite the warmth of the sunshine filtering through the trees just beginning to leaf. He hadn't been back since the funeral, and he'd run from that. His one visit to Bethany in Athens after that hadn't ended much better.

A hand slid into his and squeezed. Paisley tipped her head against his arm. "Well, this certainly brings back memories."

The image in his head expanded, like a camera pulling back for a wider-angle view. And there she was, her sun-streaked ponytail swinging, her grin flashing as she and Bethany took off for the double swing in the big oak tree.

"Yeah." Feeling more grounded, Ty tightened his hand around hers and strode toward the house.

They were early. But he had no idea how big this shindig was supposed to be, and he'd wanted a chance to speak to Bethany before everyone else arrived. Nerves hummed beneath his skin as he rang the bell and waited. The faint sounds of a female voice were answered by a deeper male tone. The door swung open to reveal one of Bethany's dads.

Dr. Gordon Bristow's dark face split into a broad smile at the sight of them. "Ty Brooks. It's good to see you, son."

"And you, sir." He accepted the firm handshake.

"And Paisley! Oh, my goodness, girl, it's been forever. Come give me a hug."

She stepped inside, giving him a squeeze and a smile. "It's great to see you, Doc."

"Come on through to the back. Bethany and Paul are fussing with the last of the setup."

They trailed him through the house. Dimly, Ty noted new paint on the walls, a new sofa, and the same ancient chair by the fireplace that Dr. Bristow's husband refused to part with. Then they were outside again, and there was Bethany, cheeks flushed and glowing, glossy black hair gleaming in the sunshine, looking happy as she argued with her father over the placement of a picnic table.

The sight of her struck Ty dumb, even when Bethany turned and saw him.

"Ty!"

He didn't know what to do with her delighted smile and was saved from figuring it out when her gaze slid over to Paisley and down to where their hands intertwined. Bethany actively squealed and danced in place before racing over to throw her arms around Paisley. They traded enthusiastic hugs and what he thought of as girl greetings, and when Bethany pulled back, her deep brown eyes were misty.

"Garrett would be so happy you two are back together." She waved a finger between them. "And don't think I'm gonna let you out of here without hearing how that happened."

Ty shifted on his feet, not knowing how to respond. He didn't know how to talk about Garrett without the clawing pain of loss.

As her father discretely slipped back into the house, Bethany reached out to clasp Ty's hand with a knowing look. "He wanted you happy."

"I know." Willing down the knot in his throat,

he tried for a smile that probably came off more like a grimace. "He wanted you happy, too."

"I am. I mean, of course, I wish he was here every day and that I wasn't doing this alone. But I'm doing what we wanted."

Ty was missing something, but he recognized her intensity. "Doing what?"

Her smile dialed up to beaming. "I'm pregnant."

If an actual bomb had gone off in the backyard, he'd have been less shocked. For several long moments, his mouth simply opened and closed with no sound. Even Paisley seemed at a loss for words.

At last, he managed, "You're...I...who?"

Bethany laughed. "It's Garrett's baby."

"But...how?" Garrett had been dead for two years.

"IVF. I've had fertility issues for years. We were going through all the treatments for more than a year before he was killed. It was my second round. There's a high rate of miscarriage. I lost three before he died. But we had two viable embryos left, and I decided to use them. This one stuck."

"Garrett's baby?" Stunned, Ty started to reach out and touch her stomach, but pulled back.

She grabbed his hand and laid it over her belly. "Garrett's baby. You're going to be an uncle."

He could feel the gentle swell of it beneath the blousy shirt that had camouflaged the bump. A sign of life. Of a hope he'd thought long extinguished. A piece of the man he'd loved as a brother all his life.

"Oh my God. Oh my God!" He scooped her up into a massive, spinning hug, then abruptly set her back down, worried he'd break her. "Are you okay? Is altitude bad for the baby? Are you feeling sick? I'll get some ginger ale. Can you have ginger ale?"

Bethany practically wheezed with laughter, her long-lashed eyes glittering, and he couldn't even care it was at his expense. He was too consumed with this bubbly, buoyant feeling in his blood. It took him a few moments to recognize the alien sensation as joy.

Paisley got in on the hug train again. "This is amazing! How far along are you?"

"A little over four months. So, I feel confident in actually announcing it. That's what today is about. I'm glad y'all got here early, though, so I could tell you first."

"What do you need?" Ty demanded. "How can I help?"

"I'm good. I've sold the house, and I'm moving

home. My dads have always wanted me to join the practice, and they're over the moon at the chance to be active grandpas. Plus, Garrett's family will want to be involved." She laid a hand on her belly. "This baby will be incredibly loved."

Already thinking about all the things he wanted to teach the kid and stories he wanted to share about Garrett, Ty's throat went thick again. "Yeah."

The doorbell rang again.

"Host duty calls." Bethany squeezed Ty's arm and brushed a kiss to his cheek. "I'm glad you're here." She looked to Paisley. "Both of you."

As they watched her walk into the house, Paisley cuddled up close. "You okay, Galahad?"

Looking at the door where Bethany disappeared, he nodded. "Yeah. I think maybe I finally am."

EPILOGUE

They were among the last to leave the party. Paisley had happily caught up with other Coopers Bend friends she hadn't seen in years, while Ty stuck close to Bethany. He was doting and ecstatic. After the added guilt she knew he'd carried about the baby she'd lost after Garrett's death, it was lovely to see. It was also intriguing.

In high school, neither of them had been thinking about children, and in their time together as adults, it certainly hadn't come up. Paisley had long ago given up on the idea of having kids. She *liked* her life, liked the one she was building with Ty. Unlike Emerson, her biological clock wasn't sounding a gong. But watching his solicitous attention to the mama to be, it was hard not to wonder whether he'd ever wanted to be a father and what it would be like to be the focus of that kind of attention.

By the time they slid into his truck, the sun was sinking below the horizon. Paisley slid off her heels and began to massage her arches. "Well, that was not at all what I was expecting of today."

"It's a helluva thing. I can't decide if she's brave or crazy, doing this on her own. I mean obviously she's not entirely on her own, but it won't be the same."

"I expect it's a little bit of brave and crazy. Although personally, I think that essentially defines parenthood in general. Still, I'm sure there will be a whole host of challenges that come up that she didn't anticipate."

"Isn't that parenthood, too?"

"True enough." Although she wondered if Bethany wouldn't have it worse. The choice to have her dead husband's baby, well after his death, was going to have tongues wagging. There'd be some who assumed it wasn't IVF and she was covering up involvement with someone else. People could be awful. But Paisley kept that to herself. No reason to dampen the joy.

Seeing her opening, she asked the question

that had been circling all afternoon. "Did you ever want that? Parenthood?"

Ty shot her a speculative look from the driver's seat.

"That's not a hint, in case you were wondering. I'm legitimately curious."

"Most of the other guys on my team talked about it often. Some of them had families and wives back home. I couldn't have done that for all the same reasons I couldn't stay with you. Since I didn't have anybody waiting on me back home anyway, it seemed a moot point. I was career military. Until I wasn't. Then I was a mess. And now, here you are again. I admit, I hadn't thought about it before. Hadn't let myself. But I wondered today."

"Me too. I don't know where I stand on kids. It's not a dealbreaker for me one way or the other. I figure we've got plenty of other details to figure out before that becomes a relevant question. I mean, we haven't even closed on the house, yet."

"Fair enough."

Happy to have her curiosity satisfied without it turning into a Thing, Paisley stretched. "In other news, did I imagine Jonathan Bane watching Bethany?"

"No, no, you did not. I was surprised he was there."

"They were friends as kids. I remember Bethany saying he grew up on the farm next door."

"Yeah, he did a lot of volunteering with the veterinary clinic back then. I think Doc Rollins mentioned he's maybe doing something with training therapy dogs now. Not sure. It's something that has him working with their practice."

"Huh."

Ty arched a brow. "What is that huh about?"

"I just wonder if he's finally going to make a move."

"What are you talking about?"

"Oh, he totally had a thing for her back in high school. But of course, he never acted on it because there was always Garrett."

"He's younger than her."

"Only by three years."

"How do you even know this?"

She offered a supercilious grin. "I had a nose for romance, even then."

"I think your romantic heart is seeing something that isn't there. She's pregnant with another man's baby. That's not exactly a prime dating situation."

"Do you think she shouldn't date?"

He considered the question. "No. No, Garrett wouldn't want her life to be over any more than he did mine. He'd want her to find someone else to love her. But that's a big, complicated mess of a situation. Lots of baggage. I don't know many—or frankly any—men who'd want to sign on for that."

"We'll see." Realizing he wasn't driving them back to the hotel, she straightened in her seat. "Where are we going?"

"Another walk down memory lane."

She knew, even before he turned toward the river, where he was headed. Apparently, this was a trip for banishing ghosts. As he parked under what she'd always thought of as their tree, she arched a brow. "Did you have plans of steaming up the windows? Because I will remind you that your truck does not have a bench seat, and it is too cold after dark to make use of your truck bed."

"As appealing as that is, no. That wasn't why I brought you out here." He turned off the truck. "Walk with me."

Wishing she'd known he wanted to walk, she slid her heels back on and joined him, taking the hand he offered. There was a well-groomed path that hadn't been there years ago. They stuck to it for a ways, lost in their own thoughts as the river burbled beside them.

"So many memories here," she murmured.

"Which ones are you thinking of?"

"The day you carved our initials in our tree. Dozens of picnics on the banks. Lazy afternoons dreaming about the future. Our first time." There were others. So very many others.

"Is it only the good ones for you?"

She understood what he was asking. "It is now." And why shouldn't she hang on to those beautiful memories, when the boy who'd given them to her had grown into the man by her side?

He pulled her to a stop, tugging her back against his chest and faced them toward the river. "This place was important to us. But we never came back after that day."

She didn't have to ask which day and didn't think he needed her confirmation.

"I feel like I ruined it for us."

At the self-recrimination in his voice, she stroked her free hand down his arm. "You did what you had to do. I don't hold it against this place."

"Did you ever come back here without me?"

"No. It would have hurt too bad." She leaned back against him, soaking in the comfort of his nearness. "I'm happy to be here with you now."

"Me too. And that's part of why I brought you. Because I wanted to do something to reclaim this place for good memories."

"Oh?" Where was he going with this?

Turning her to face him, he skimmed the hair back from her face. "I love you Paisley Ann Parish. I love your laugh, your smile, and how you make everything more fun. I love your romantic's view of the world and how it keeps me from dwelling too long in the dark. I love that stubborn streak that meant you never gave up on me, even when I probably deserved it."

Lifting both hands, he brushed a kiss over her knuckles that had her halfway to swooning. "You've been it for me since that kiss at the homecoming dance all those years ago. I knew it then, and I'm doing now what you thought I was that day the last time we came here." He dropped to one knee. "Marry me."

Paisley's hand flew to her mouth. "Oh my God. Are you serious?"

He slipped out a ring box from his pocket and flipped it open.

She squeaked. That was a real, shiny engagement ring in there. In his hand. Where he knelt on the ground. The ache in her feet told her in no uncertain terms she was definitely awake and not dreaming this whole thing.

And here she'd thought Bethany's baby announcement was going to be the biggest shock of the day.

"We spent a lot of years apart. Years that showed me in no uncertain terms that life is short. I wasted a lot of time feeling unworthy and broken. You changed that. In a very real way, you brought me back to life, and I don't want to lose another minute with you. So marry me, Paisley."

She considered herself a practical romantic. It was the small, everyday things that usually did her in. Much as she loved them, she didn't expect or want grand gestures. Flashy wasn't her style. So, that he'd brought her here, where they'd had so many of their firsts, to ask her to be his and heal the wound of their previous, painful end, was exactly right. He was exactly right and exactly hers. Finally.

Tears burned her eyes, and she swallowed against the emotion in her throat to find her voice and give him a sassy smile. "Well, since you *asked* so nicely..."

"I did promise to work on the bossy thing. Sorry about that. Paisley, will you—"

She pressed a finger to his lips. "I think you can get away with orders just this once. Because the answer is yes. For you, the answer will always be yes."

His answering grin lit up the night. "Then let's make it official." Pulling the ring from the box, he slid it onto her finger.

A perfect fit.

As he rose and slipped his arms around her, she linked her hands behind his neck. "You know...Tennessee is a no-waiting-period state for marriage licenses."

"Oh? Do I even want to know why you know that?"

"The same reason I know most random trivia. Book research. I'm just saying, Gatlinburg is only a three-hour drive. We could swing by on our way home. In the name of not losing any more time."

His delighted laugh warmed her already over-flowing heart. "Have I mentioned I love the way you think?"

"Once or twice, but a girl never gets tired of hearing it."

"I'll keep that in mind."

And with the moon rising behind them, she kissed the first love she was going to marry.

GET YOUR BONUS CONTENT!

Because I'm a major plotter, it is only once in a very great while that I have any actual deleted scenes from my books. It just so happens that I ended up cutting a scene that didn't quite fit the pacing of the book, but it absolutely shows the lighter side of Ty. Get your copy here: https://kait-nolan.com/made-for-loving-you-deleted-scene/

CHOOSE YOUR NEXT ROMANCE

I HOPE you enjoyed this conclusion to the Rescue My Heart trilogy! If you'd like to read all about Emerson and Caleb (and see where Paisley first made it onto the page), then their hot, younger best friend, firefighter next door, empty nest romance is the book for you. Check out *Let It Be Me,* the first of the Men of the Misfit Inn series.

If you want more Ari, she features heavily in the books of all her aunts, beginning with *When You Got A Good Thing,* Kennedy and Xander's story. Theirs is another second chance romance that's sure to warm the cockles of your heart.

OTHER BOOKS BY KAIT NOLAN

A complete and up-to-date list of all my books can be found at https://kaitnolan.com.

KILTED HEARTS
SMALL TOWN CONTEMPORARY SCOTTISH ROMANCE

- *Jilting The Kilt* (prequel)
- *Cowboy in a Kilt* (Raleigh and Kyla)
- *Grump in a Kilt* (Malcolm and Charlotte)
- *Playboy in a Kilt* (Connor and Sophie)
- *Protector in a Kilt* (Ewan and Isobel)
- *Single Dad in a Kilt* (Hamish and Afton)

BAD BOY BAKERS

SMALL TOWN MILITARY ROMANCE

- *Rescued By a Bad Boy* (Brax and Mia prequel)
- *Mixed Up With a Marine* (Brax and Mia)
- *Wrapped Up with a Ranger* (Holt and Cayla)
- *Stirred Up by a SEAL* (Jonah and Rachel)
- *Hung Up on the Hacker* (Cash and Hadley)
- *Caught Up with the Captain* (Grey and Rebecca)

RESCUE MY HEART SERIES
SMALL TOWN MILITARY ROMANCE

- *Someone Like You* (Ivy and Harrison)
- *What I Like About You* (Laurel and Sebastian)
- *Bad Case of Loving You* (Paisley and Ty prequel) Included in *Made For Loving You* (Paisley and Ty)

THE MISFIT INN SERIES
SMALL TOWN FAMILY ROMANCE

- *When You Got A Good Thing* (Kennedy and Xander)
- *Til There Was You* (Misty and Denver)
- *Those Sweet Words* (Pru and Flynn)
- *Stay A Little Longer* (Athena and Logan)
- *Bring It On Home* (Maggie and Porter)
- *Come Away with Me* (Moses and Zuri)

MEN OF THE MISFIT INN
SMALL TOWN SOUTHERN ROMANCE

- *Let It Be Me* (Emerson and Caleb)
- *Our Kind of Love* (Abbey and Kyle)
- *Don't You Wanna Stay* (Deanna and Wyatt)
- *Until We Meet Again* (Samantha and Griffin prequel)
- *Come A Little Closer* (Samantha and Griffin)
- *Just Wanted You To Know* (Livia and Declan)

WISHFUL ROMANCE SERIES
SMALL TOWN SOUTHERN ROMANCE

- *Once Upon A Coffee* (Avery and Dillon)
- *To Get Me To You* (Cam and Norah)

- *Know Me Well* (Liam and Riley)
- *Be Careful, It's My Heart* (Brody and Tyler)
- *Just For This Moment* (Myles and Piper)
- *Wish I Might* (Reed and Cecily)
- *Turn My World Around* (Tucker and Corinne)
- *Dance Me A Dream* (Jace and Tara)
- *See You Again* (Trey and Sandy)
- *The Christmas Fountain* (Chad and Mary Alice)
- *You Were Meant For Me* (Mitch and Tess)
- *A Lot Like Christmas* (Ryan and Hannah)
- *Dancing Away With My Heart* (Zach and Lexi)

WISHING FOR A HERO SERIES (A WISHFUL SPINOFF SERIES)
SMALL TOWN ROMANTIC SUSPENSE

- *Make You Feel My Love* (Judd and Autumn)
- *Watch Over Me* (Nash and Rowan)
- *Can't Take My Eyes Off You* (Ethan and Miranda)
- *Burn For You* (Sean and Delaney)

MEET CUTE ROMANCE
SMALL TOWN SHORT ROMANCE

- *Once Upon A Snow Day*
- *Once Upon A New Year's Eve*
- *Once Upon An Heirloom*
- *Once Upon A Coffee*
- *Once Upon A Campfire*
- *Once Upon A Rescue*

SUMMER CAMP
CONTEMPORARY ROMANCE

- *Once Upon A Campfire*
- *Second Chance Summer*

ABOUT KAIT

Kait is a Mississippi native, who often swears like a sailor, calls everyone sugar, honey, or darlin', and can wield a bless your heart like a saber or a Snuggie, depending on requirements.

You can find more information on this *USA Today* best selling and RITA ® Award-winning au-

thor and her books on her website http://kait
nolan.com.

Do you need more small town sass and spark?
Sign up for <u>her newsletter</u> to hear about new re-
leases, book deals, and exclusive content!

www.ingramcontent.com/pod-product-compliance
Lightning Source LLC
Chambersburg PA
CBHW060230100726
47907CB00003B/576